Andrew's Key
Stories From Hartford

Amanda Hamm

ISBN: 978-098506595-9

Chapter 1

I kept the door locked because I couldn't figure out why it was locked. It seemed completely unnecessary. A dark skeleton key hung on a metal hook only about a foot above the handle. I had been in the house for two weeks and hadn't yet had the courage to use that key. There was no rush and that's what I told myself each time I considered checking out the second floor. The old door was at the bottom of the stairs and I had decided that today was the day I would go through it.

My ear pressed against the cool wood of the door. It was a tiny bit of relief against the otherwise stifling house. It was June and there was no air conditioning. I hoped I'd be used to the heat by August. All I could hear was my own breathing, which was deliberately calm. I had heard noises above me... noises that suggested someone or something was moving around up there.

At first I thought it was my imagination. It was a bright, beautiful sunny afternoon though and things that went bump in the night normally went bump in the *night*. That was how I knew there was a perfectly rational explanation. My best guess was that some sort of wild animal, maybe a squirrel, had somehow gotten in the house. Maybe there was a broken window. If there was an animal and/or a broken window upstairs, those were things I should probably do something about. A grownup would fix a problem with her house and I was supposed to be figuring out how to be a grownup.

The first thing I did was walk around the outside of the house. The windows all appeared to be intact. The sun got in my eyes on one side though and made it difficult to be certain. The next thing I did was head into the garage to pick up the biggest, heaviest, sturdiest weapon I could find. It was a shovel so big I needed two hands to carry it. I wasn't wild about taking the dirty old thing into the house, but if something up there wanted to give me rabies I intended to put up a fight.

I propped open the back door as I came inside. My plan was to chase whatever it was outside and I needed to be sure it had an exit. I listened at the locked door for a full minute and didn't hear anything behind it.

"Here we go," I whispered to myself. I rested the shovel on the ground so I could support it with one hand and took down the key with my free hand. The keyhole was rather large and yet it took a few tries to fit the key into it because my hands were shaking. I was about to turn the key when I heard a voice.

It was a weak male voice that said only, "Rose?"

Animals did not have voices. I slowly pulled the key back out and put it back on the hook where I watched in shock as it swung from side to side. Then the voice called out again a little stronger, "Rose?"

The shovel hit the floor with a terrifying clatter and I was out the back door before it stopped vibrating. I jumped into my car before I realized that I had no keys. I ran back inside without thinking and grabbed my backpack off the counter. I didn't have any idea where I was going to go. The only thing I knew for sure was that animals did not talk.

I drove down the narrow country road about a mile, just looking for someplace I could stop and think. I pulled into the remains of a driveway where a house must have once stood. My heart was pounding so fast I could hear the blood in my ears. Even grownups could ask for help sometimes so I pulled out my phone. There was no one I could call. I looked up the number for the local police. As soon as I hung up, I drove home and pulled into my own driveway. I sat in my car with it still running and stared at the house. It was large, especially for one person, and square and brick. It was set back a bit from the street with a long driveway on the side and detached white garage behind it. My dad had come out and mowed the grass just before I moved in. It was getting tall again and that was something else I was going to have to figure out eventually. I knew there was a lawn mower in the garage, but I had never used a lawn mower.

A black and white police car crunched on the gravel next to me and I immediately felt safe enough to turn off my engine. And a tiny bit embarrassed. I had never called the police before. I got out and met the two officers. One was very young. I hoped he was not quite as young as he looked because if he hadn't been wearing a uniform I'd have guessed he was still in high school. The other officer appeared to be in his forties. It was the younger one who addressed me, in a voice much deeper than I expected.

"Did you report a possible intruder?" he asked.

2

"Yes, sir."

"You're Rebecca Hilson?"

"Yes."

"And this is your house?"

I nodded and said, "Yes," again.

"Can you tell us what happened?"

"I, um, I thought I heard someone moving around upstairs, like footsteps. But I don't know how anyone could have gotten up there. I'm beginning to wonder if I imagined it." That was a lie. What happened still felt very real to me. I had this feeling, however, that they weren't going to find anything.

"We'll check it out. Is the house unlocked now?"

"Yeah, the front and back doors are open," I said. "There's a door on the far side that should still be locked. I don't have a key for that one."

The older officer said, "You wait here," as they both began to walk towards the house.

I nodded and watched as they split up and walked around the house. Soon one went in the front door and one went in the back. It felt as though they were in there for a long time. A memory of my dad's older sister came to me. She found me sitting alone when our house was full of people after my grandmother's funeral. She had pulled a rosary out of her pocket and said, "The rosary is a wonderful tool for strong emotions, dear. It helps to bring them and it helps to calm them."

Her logic was still lost on me, but I latched onto the word "calm." I reached into my open car window and pulled a rosary out of a side pocket on my backpack. I was in the habit of holding the beads bunched up in my fists as I moved through them. I wasn't really hiding what I was doing, just didn't need to advertise it. I had been told that only old people prayed the rosary anymore. The familiar feel of the beads in my hands and the words in my head did provide some comfort. The sight of the officers emerging from my back door alone completed the sensation.

I slipped the rosary into my left hand and moved that hand behind my back as the policemen approached. This time the older one did most of the talking. "We couldn't find anyone in the house. There's an outside door and an inside door at the bottom of the steps and they were both locked. We opened the inside door to take a look upstairs

3

and checked everywhere that seemed big enough for a person to hide. It looks clear. If there was someone up there, he must have left."

I nodded, more because I expected the news than because I accepted it.

"Would you like to go inside and see if anything is missing or damaged?"

"No, I wouldn't even know if anything was missing. I just moved in."

The younger officer gave me a funny look. "You don't remember what you brought with you?"

"No, I… I inherited the house from my aunt. Almost everything inside belonged to her. I haven't had a chance to… you know?"

They both seemed to understand and the older one said, "Oh, Rose Hilson was your aunt?"

"Yeah, she was."

"I'm sorry for your loss, ma'am. Ms. Hilson was a real nice lady."

"Thank you. I wish I had known her better myself." That was true. I thought if I had been closer to her, I wouldn't feel so guilty for having all of her possessions.

"Well, do you feel safe going inside or do you want us to hang around for a bit?"

Embarrassment was taking over again so I quickly shook my head. "No, I'll be fine. I'm sure you guys were thorough and I'm sorry if I wasted your time."

"Glad to help, ma'am. You have a nice day."

The younger man waved to me as the two of them climbed back into their car. I walked directly into my house without looking back. If they were watching, I wanted them to see someone who felt safe. Once inside though, I just stood by the back door not knowing how to actually feel safe.

I needed something to do. The first thing that occurred to me was that I had left my backpack and keys in my car. And that the windows were down. There was also a shovel to return to the garage and, oh yeah, a whole house full of stuff that I was supposed to be organizing. I got my car and unused weapon in order and found myself again facing that locked wooden door. Two policemen had just inspected my upstairs. When would it ever feel safer?

I grabbed the key before I could talk myself out of it. Even with steady hands, it took a moment to get it unlocked. A skeleton key was something else I had never used. I pulled the door open slowly.

4

Cheery sunshine greeted me through the window on the outside door opposite the landing. The sight was vaguely familiar, which helped me relax. I had been upstairs a few times as a kid and even once slept in one of those bedrooms though I couldn't remember why.

The house first belonged to my grandparents. My dad's dad died before I was born and his mom died when I was nine. My aunt Rose lived with her mom for about a year before her death and stayed in the house afterward. She felt something like a stand-in grandmother after that.

I gingerly placed my foot on the bottom step. Then I sprinted up the rest of them sort of like ripping off a band-aid. At the top of the stairs and to the right was a bathroom. It looked mostly as I remembered it. An old claw-footed tub sat on one side. It hadn't been used in so long that spider webs made lace around the claws and some of the inside. I did not immediately notice any inhabitants. I still sort of wished I had that giant shovel handy.

On the edge of the sink sat a dish of still unused soaps. The tiny pastel pieces were formed into roses. They were faded and grayed by a layer of dust. I remembered wanting to use them as a child and being told they were only for company. I reached out to pick one up and discovered that they had melted together. I set down the depressing clump and moved out of the bathroom.

There were four other doors in the hallway. Three were open to bedrooms. The one closed door was uncommonly skinny and led to an attic. I had already conquered one flight of stairs and planned to investigate only the bedrooms. The first had basic bedroom furniture – a double bed with a wedding ring quilt, a wide dresser with six drawers, a small bedside table and a standing mirror. I walked over to the mirror and took a look at myself. I looked like a rational person. Mostly. I was wearing basic gray shorts and a pink v-neck t-shirt. My hair was light brown and dropped below my shoulders when it was down. At the moment, it was pulled back in my default French braid style. It was simple and convenient yet I hoped still conveyed a sense that I had made an effort.

I tried to smile at my reflection. The effort didn't quite work so I turned my attention to the mirror itself. Despite a bit of dust, the wood was beautiful. It had intricate swirls carved on the frame and the supports and had a slight reddish tint. I made my first decision about the house. This mirror I would keep. It would eventually go in my bedroom. I would need to figure out what eventually meant later.

5

I moved to the dresser and began opening drawers. They were all full of clothes, women's clothes. I didn't know if they had belonged to my aunt or my grandmother. They'd be equally useless to me either way. Rose was tall like her father and about six inches taller than I was. My grandmother I remembered as being more than a bit plump. I would go through them all later to be sure before I donated them somewhere. I checked the bedside table next. It had one drawer and a single pencil rolled to the front as I opened it. An old matchbook was the only other thing in the drawer.

I opened the closet next and came face to face with a wall of cardboard. The boxes were stacked three deep clear to the ceiling and as far as I could tell none of them were labeled. I made another decision. Don't open any more closets today.

My stomach growled. It must have been nearing dinnertime. Feeding myself had begun to feel like a chore lately so I sometimes put it off. I took only a quick peek into the other two bedrooms. The first had a pair of twin beds, stripped and shoved against the far wall. There was a stack of boxes in the corner that I could only assume didn't fit in the closet. The last bedroom had a hodgepodge of stuff I couldn't fully appreciate with only a cursory glance. Mostly I noticed that the walls were painted a light purple while the rest of the house was white. There seemed to be several dressers and other types of furniture, several floor lamps, more boxes, something that might be an old-fashioned sewing machine, more boxes and rolls of what I guessed were rugs or carpet remnants. I didn't see a bed, but couldn't rule out the possibility there was one under some of the boxes.

When I reached the bottom of the stairs, I confirmed that the outside door was still locked. I closed the inside door and grabbed the key. I stopped before I put the key in the lock. Why did Aunt Rose keep this door locked with the key so convenient? It was a question I still could not answer. If I was going to live in this house, I would need to conquer my fear of the unknown. Besides, I now knew what was upstairs and unpleasant or not there was nothing sinister about a ton of work. I hung the key on the hook and opened the door wide against the wall. The steps weren't scary at all with the sunlight streaming across the landing. I felt comfortable enough to find something to eat.

Chapter 2

I had trouble sleeping the night after I heard the voice. It only continued my streak of restless nights since moving into the old house. I began my day as usual with a simple bowl of cereal. I was trying to form a routine for my days. Any life needs a bit of structure so I hoped a solid routine would begin to feel like living a life. I washed my face and put on some running clothes. Every morning except Sunday I ran the almost two and a half miles into town.

First I checked my phone and found two voicemails. The first was from my mother. It said, "Becky, honey, we just heard that the police were at your house. Is everything all right? Please let us know how you're doing. Please, we really want to hear from you. Give me a call, okay?"

The second was from my father. "Hi, honey. We just heard that you had to call the cops. If you're not ready to talk, just send a quick text that you're okay so we don't worry. Thanks, honey."

I had a pretty good idea who their source was. Dad was right. I wasn't ready to talk. I knew it made me seem like a sullen teenager. But I wasn't ready. I replied to his message with a text that said: Don't worry, Dad. I'm fine.

Mom would read it, too.

I put in my earbuds as soon as I got outside and paced up and down my driveway for a warm-up. After some quick stretches, I was off. It was a straight line to Hartford and I could mostly run on the grass next to the road. There was very little traffic on the road as usual. The trees along the path were very green and tall enough that I never had to duck under any branches. So far this route was my favorite part of the move.

I slowed to a walk as I reached that office building with a weird purple stripe on the front. I went into the small grocery store a block to the left. I walked up to the donut case first. I was on a health food kick and donuts were not on the menu, but I could look. Then I picked out a few bananas and a few peaches and went up front to pay

7

for them. I was only one person and I came to the store nearly every morning so I didn't need to get much each trip.

"Good morning, Mabel," I said to the short round woman behind the register. She had dark gray hair in a long thin braid that went all the way to her waist. I guessed her to be in her late fifties and that she knew more about me than I even guessed about her.

"Morning, Rebecca. How are you, hon? I heard about your little scare yesterday."

"It was nothing really," I tried to assure her. Her knowledge meant that I was probably right about who had been talking to my parents. I wasn't upset with her though. I believed she meant well.

"They couldn't find anything, huh?" she asked.

"I probably imagined it."

"I don't know, hon. Haven't I been telling you that place is haunted?"

She had been telling me that. And she was not the only one. People in town, however, insisted that my new home was haunted by a little girl, not an old man. I said, "And I keep telling you that I haven't seen any signs of your ghost."

"Well, I don't think Jimmy would mind checking your place for you again. That boy is sweet on you already."

I hoped she meant the younger officer, but thought it best to change the subject either way. If I asked which one was Jimmy, Mabel would be reporting my interest all over town. "What else is going on?" I asked.

"Oh, you know, I heard Michelle's boy is going to be staying with his granddad this weekend."

The only thing this news meant to me was that we weren't talking about me anymore. Therefore, it was good news. I nodded appreciatively.

"And Jack and Jill are expecting a little one. Isn't that wonderful?"

"You actually told me that yesterday, but I haven't been over there to congratulate her yet. I might do that right now."

"Okay, I'll see you soon, hon."

I waved as I left. The first few times I bought groceries there, it had seemed odd to complete the transaction without such trivial things as telling me how much my purchases cost and acknowledging that I had paid for them. But I had gotten used to talking about everything else instead.

8

A block from the grocery store was a place called "Things to Do." It had become my second most common stop, though I had yet to actually buy anything there. I was pretty sure that getting a life was going to include getting a hobby. I couldn't decide on one. The woman who ran the shop was becoming the closest thing I had to a friend in town. She seemed just as excited about "finding my passion" as I was. Honestly, she might have been more excited.

There was a loud jingling sound as I opened the door, like a flock of wind chimes taking flight. Jill came rushing over to meet me. "I'm so glad you're here," she said. "I've had a brainstorm."

"Okay. Let me hear it."

"Wait, wait. We've got to get you in the right frame of mind. Come all the way in." Jill grabbed the side of my arm and gently pulled me towards the back of her shop. "Now," she said, "close your eyes."

I did as I was told and took a few more steps as she led me forward.

"Picture yourself in your favorite room in your house," she continued.

It was a bit more difficult to follow that instruction as I didn't yet have a favorite room. In fact, the only room that popped into my head was that cobweb covered bathroom. I was probably not going to be practicing any hobbies in that room. I nodded dutifully anyway.

Jill's voice was going up an octave. "You're relaxed and happy and losing track of time as you work on a fabulous creation in… open your eyes… clay!"

When I opened my eyes, Jill had her arms splayed Vanna White style next to a display of pottery tools. I tried not to look as put off as I felt. "I'm not sure," I said.

She didn't appear remotely disappointed. "We want you to be sure," she said. "You keep thinking about it and let's go ahead and look around a bit."

I turned to look at the next shelf, which had some paint by number kits. One with a tiger was kind of pretty, but certainly beyond my capabilities. "By the way," I said, "Mabel tells me that you and Jack have some news."

Jill grinned sheepishly. "Yeah, we're due around Thanksgiving."

"Congratulations!"

"And I am determined to find your passion before then."

"I hope so. But in the meantime, I'll take this today." I picked up a box of markers and handed it to her.

9

"Drawing?" she asked hopefully.

"I don't think so. I found a whole bunch of unlabeled boxes yesterday so I'm thinking those will come in handy."

"Maybe it'll start something." Jill took the markers to her register. I said goodbye to her and put the markers in my backpack with my fruit. It was time to go home.

I always ran to town, focusing on nothing but my music and the rhythm of my feet hitting the ground. The return trip I took at a walk. It was hotter and there were regularly things in my backpack that I didn't want to jostle. Even though I still listened to music, it didn't push aside thoughts when I went at a slower pace.

All the thoughts that vied for position in my brain came from the last year of my life. My first 24 years had been reasonably smooth sailing and then things started to happen. Aunt Rose had died about eight months ago. I mostly saw her on holidays and while I enjoyed her company she wasn't a major part of my life. That is, until she died and left everything to me. I could not escape the connection now. For a long time I had tried to pretend there wasn't a house full of stuff with my name on it.

Two months after that, Jacob told me that he wouldn't wait anymore. We had been together for nearly five years and he had proposed twice. I kept telling him that we didn't need to hurry. I was still in grad school after all. He was done with school after four years and was working full time. Two weeks before Christmas we had a long talk. He said that he wanted to give me an engagement ring for Christmas and that he wanted it to mean that we would make plans for a wedding as soon as I graduated. I told him I couldn't commit to that. He told me our relationship was over.

I finished my MBA as planned. Two days later I had another conversation that shook things up. My parents asked what I had planned next. I said I wasn't sure, that I was thinking of pursuing another degree as soon as I decided which one. They said that was very interesting. Those were their exact words, "That's very interesting, honey." Then my mom started crying, sobbing really, and didn't stop until she came to the end of a big speech about how she had failed me as a mother, how I didn't know how to live a life, how I was scared to grow up. And she confessed out of the blue that they had suffered three miscarriages and a stillbirth before I came along and that was why she held on so tightly. I felt as though she was blaming me for tragedies I hadn't even known about.

Then my dad took over and explained their plan for letting go. He said they had already made some phone calls and had the utilities turned back on at *my* house. He said that as painful as it might be for all three of us, I had two weeks to pack my things and move out. He said all I needed to be a successful adult was some emotional independence. That's what I was looking for among all the boxes and stuff left in the house that now belonged to me more fully than they had for the past eight months.

I wasn't pouting when I stopped speaking to my parents. I was trying to figure out how to give them what they wanted. I was trying to figure out how to stop being a disappointment to them. The answer must be somewhere in that house. I watched it come into view as I passed two large trees in the side yard. Home sweet home.

I locked the front door behind myself and hung up my backpack. I was unzipping it when I realized that there was a man sitting in my living room. He looked at me strangely and said, "You're not Rose."

Chapter 3

I thought the man might be even older than my dad who was 71. He had kind eyes that showed confusion and even a little bit of fear. Though I was startled and at least as confused as he seemed, I didn't feel threatened. I shook my head slowly. "My name is Rebecca," I said.

He looked around himself for a moment. "Where is Rose?"

"She's not here. I'm her niece."

"Rose and I have tea at 10:30," he said.

The man didn't seem to know that my aunt had died. How had no one told him in eight months? I didn't want to be the one to break the news. "Rose isn't here," I repeated.

His eyes clouded before he looked down at his hands. "I miss Rose."

Maybe he did know. He seemed lost somehow, perhaps lost in his own head. There were no couches in the room, only six squashy recliners in various shades of beige all surrounding a long, shiny coffee table. I sat down in the chair to his left. "My name is Rebecca. Rose was my aunt and I live here now."

"Rebecca?" he looked at me with a hint of recognition. "You're Frank's girl?"

I nodded. "Yeah, Frank is my dad."

He looked at me intently for a moment. I didn't see as much confusion in his expression. "You look so much like your aunt when she was your age. She was beautiful, too. Turned all the heads, she did. Bet you have your share of admirers as well."

Now the old guy was making me blush. "Sir, what is your name?"

"My name is Andrew Lately. You can call me Andrew. I won't have any more of this sir business." His voice was stern, but he was smiling.

"Yes, s- Andrew," I said. I felt as though I had heard that name before. The fact that he was a friend of Rose's made me even more comfortable with him. I wanted to ask him how he got into my house though. I knew both doors were locked and if there was some sort of secret entrance to my house that I didn't know about, well, I wanted to know about it. I wasn't sure how to ask gently. I didn't like how he looked when he was afraid of me. "Do you live nearby, Andrew?"

He smiled at me. "When we were young, it would have been a five-minute walk right down that street." He tilted his head in the opposite direction of my morning run to town. "It takes a guy like me a bit longer. I can still do it without a cane anyway. I'm not being stubborn now mind. I'd use one if it came to that. I'm just grateful that I can do it on my own for now."

"I'm a little thirsty. Can I get you a glass of water while I'm up?" I hoped he didn't mention tea again. Water and a little milk for my cereal were the only drinks I had in the house.

Andrew nodded at me. "That's awfully nice of you, dear. I'd love a glass of water."

"I'll be right back." I dashed to the kitchen and brought back two full glasses as quickly as I could. I handed one to him and reclaimed my seat.

"Thank you, um… I'm sorry," he said. "I seem to have forgotten your name."

"It's Rebecca."

"I'm afraid I've been very forgetful lately." He started laughing to himself. "Maybe people will start calling me Forgetful Lately, instead of Andrew, huh?" I wasn't sure what to say to that, but he shrugged it off before it became awkward that I didn't answer. "Anyway," he continued, "you'll have to forgive me if I ask your name again."

"That's okay. I'll tell you my name as many times as you ask for it."

"You're a sweet girl. Just like your aunt. Rose was just… Did she ever tell you about the time she got my clothes back for me?"

I shook my head. My aunt always struck me as a pretty straight-laced woman. I was pretty sure I'd remember a story about some guy missing his clothes.

Andrew chuckled softly to himself. "I was about sixteen and Rose was a year younger. It was a real hot day in August. Must have been triple digits. Me and William, that's my kid brother, we decided to take a swim with two of our friends in the pond off Miller's Road. The four of us stripped down to our skivvies and jumped right in. It cooled us right off and we were having a fine time, until that is we noticed that someone had run off with our clothes. They must have thought it was going to be pretty funny when the four of us boys had

13

to march through town in nothing but our underpants. And that might have been funny, but William and me, we knew there'd be a switch waiting for us if we showed up at home missing our clothes. We didn't have all that many to spare you know. Our friends figured pretty much the same thing. So the four of us sat in that pond trying to think our way out of the mess. Then we saw Rose running towards us like the very angel of mercy. She brought our clothes back to us, dropped the whole pile next to the pond and took off again without an explanation. We found out later it was the Hamilton girls behind the prank. They were friends with Rose and when she found out what they had done, well, she probably saved those girls from a heap of trouble, too, if their parents had found out." Andrew put his glass to his lips when he finished and drank half the water in one gulp.

I had been sipping mine while enjoying his story.

"Now," he said, "tell me something about yourself."

I shrugged, not sure what to say.

"What do you like to do?"

"Well, I run in the mornings." I felt as though the most important thing about myself at the moment was an explanation as to why I wasn't exactly fit for company.

"Nothing else you do?"

"I just finished school and I can't figure out what sort of job I want."

"No hobbies either?"

"Not yet. Do you know Jill from the craft store in town?"

"The craft store?" Andrew looked thoughtful. "Doesn't James' daughter run that?"

I nodded because it seemed as though he might know what he was talking about. Everyone in town over a certain age referred to everyone under a certain age as so-and-so's son or daughter. If I hung around long enough, maybe I could connect all the dots. "Well, Jill thinks she's going to help me find my passion."

Andrew tilted his head at me. "What's your name again?"

"Rebecca."

"Well, Rebecca, hobbies are great and I hope James' daughter can help you find something you enjoy. But remember this… passion should be saved for the Lord and His people."

"Something tells me I *will* remember that." His observation made a lot of sense to me. Maybe I was having so much trouble picking a hobby because I was expecting too much from it.

"You know what I remember...?" Andrew said. "Another time William and I narrowly avoided trouble. That boy was always getting into one thing or another and since I was older it'd be my fault for not steering him right. But I tell you what... there was no steering that boy."

Andrew sighed and I waited expectantly for another story.

"We were supposed to feed them, that was all. The Thorpes, they had a hutch of rabbits. Three of them. One time they went away for the weekend and asked me and William to go over there and feed them. We were to give them some food and fresh water. That's exactly what we did the first day. But the second day, William noticed a stack of newspapers in the barn and got it into his head that we could also clean out the hutch. I think he must have been about six or seven and before I could stop him, he had plucked all three rabbits out and was pulling out the soiled paper. Now we got fresh paper in there no problem and I thought maybe he actually had a good idea."

Andrew gave me a look, one that clearly meant that the rest had only been setup and now it was time for the real story. "Then we tried to get the rabbits back into the hutch. We chased those critters all afternoon. The ornery things never even left the yard. They kept hopping in circles and twitching their little faces like they were laughing at us. We tried to work together, William trying to chase them towards me so I could catch them. It was no use. Eventually I did catch one and stuffed him back where he belonged. I got another pretty soon after that and started to think I had got the hang of it. But that last one, he wouldn't let me get near him for nothing. Pretty soon it was getting close to supper time. William and I needed to be home before Mama needed us to put the plates on the table, otherwise we'd be in for it. So we were getting kind of worried. William suggested we leave the rabbit and try to catch him after supper. But I didn't think we could risk it getting lost. You know how Mrs. Thorpe was, right, Rose? She's not the kind of woman to let a good deed go unpunished. So there we were sweating it and William managed to grab hold of that last rabbit by his hind leg. It twisted around and bit William, but he held on anyway and got the thing tucked away. And then we *ran*. We ran hard and got back to the house just as Mama was about to look for us. We couldn't have cut it any closer."

Andrew had been very animated as he remembered chasing the rabbits and he had me laughing. He looked suddenly very tired as he finished. Our glasses were both empty and I wondered if I should offer him a refill. He turned his tired eyes back to me. "Your mom and dad never gave you any siblings, did they?"

I shook my head.

"And Rose didn't give you any cousins."

That was more an observation than a question, but I shook my head again anyway. Aunt Rose had never married.

"What about your mama's family?" he asked.

"I don't… I don't know any of them very well."

Andrew wrinkled his eyes at me. "They don't live close?"

"They mostly do actually, but…" I wasn't sure how to explain the emotional distance. He looked as though he wanted me to try and it did seem to be my turn to talk. "My parents were a little older when I was born, 44 and 45. My mom is the baby of her family so when I was little her siblings – she has three of them – were sending their kids off to college or welcoming grandchildren and I think the different stages made her feel sort of disconnected from them. The cousin closest to me in age is 14 years older than me so I always sort of felt like a generation unto myself."

"And you can't relate to someone of a different age? You're talking to an old guy just fine right now." He winked at me.

"I guess so. It's just… It's different when you're a kid."

"Ah, but you're not a kid anymore."

I tried to acknowledge his point with my expression. I could reach out to some of those relatives now that I was older. Mostly I thought it was very interesting that Andrew recognized me as a grownup. Perhaps it wouldn't be long before others agreed with him. I was considering what to say when my stomach talked for me. It let out a loud gurgling sound. Andrew noticed.

"Land's sakes!" he exclaimed. "Look at the time. Here I am intruding on your lunch and you didn't even expect company, did you?" His face filled with confusion again. I thought perhaps he was realizing that he didn't know any better than I did how he had ended up in my living room. He looked around for a moment. I wondered if I should be concerned about him getting home okay. I didn't know where he lived though.

"Well," he said, "if I could trouble you one more minute for the use of your restroom, I'll just get out of your hair after that."

"It's right over here," I said as I stood and pointed out the restroom. It seemed polite to point it out even though I thought he must already know.

16

When he emerged from the restroom, I intended to walk him to the front door. Instead, he walked back to the living room and I followed him towards the side door by the stairs. He thanked me for the companionship and waved as he went through the side door. Then I watched as he solved several mysteries for me all at once by locking it behind himself.

Chapter 4

As soon as Andrew was out of sight, I closed the door at the bottom of the stairs and used the old skeleton key to secure it. I was sure that I didn't have anything to fear from the sweet man, but I didn't want to be surprised by him again. It occurred to me that if I'd walked home much faster, I might have had a confused old man wandering around my house while I was in the shower.

Once I was clean and fed, I went into my bedroom to work. So far it was the only room that was starting to feel like mine. Most of my aunt's clothes were sitting in garbage bags on the dining room table waiting for me to drop them at a thrift store. The closet and the large chest of drawers were pretty well in order. My clothes filled them only half as much as Rose's had. There was a small side table by the bed that I intended to tackle next.

I had peeked once before and knew it was mostly full of books and papers. Now it was time to make some decisions about which books or papers I should keep. I opened the bottom drawer first. It was stuffed to the very top. There were a few odds and ends mixed in with the books, mostly to make the drawer seem extra messy. The books were classics, some I hadn't read. I set the books aside as I looked through them, knowing I'd put them right back in the drawer but hoping neater stacks would make me feel as though I accomplished something. There was one recent title and I noticed a public library sticker on the back. I tried to think of that as good news. The next time I was bored I would have an errand to run.

Also in the drawer were a few blank postcards and a box of green swirl stationery. The pens next to it were nice. I had occasionally read letters Aunt Rose sent to my parents, but I could not remember any that had been addressed specifically to me. I felt a stab of guilt as I considered that I had never written to her either.

The top drawer contained the largest bible I had ever seen. It had a padded ivory cover and as I pulled it onto my lap I decided that it might also be the heaviest bible I had ever held. Inside the front cover was a record of family births. I could tell by the handwriting that it had been completed by several different people. The first few entries were people born in the eighteen hundreds. The last name on the list was mine. Above my name in the same hand it said "Baby Boy Hilson." The birth date was a little more than a year before mine and the same date was listed in the death column.

My dad was the next name. I knew there had been no additions – no lasting additions – to the family in the 45 years between him and me, but there was something about seeing it in print that made me feel very alone. I wondered how different my childhood might have been if my brother, the one I hadn't even known about a few weeks earlier, had survived.

It didn't surprise me that my parents hadn't mentioned him to me. Though I was a product of my parents' relationship, I knew I wasn't part of that relationship. I had always been an extra person in the house. Always loved, always wanted and even cherished, but always extra. I missed my parents and though I knew they missed me, I also knew they still had each other.

I felt myself growing a little depressed. And looking back at the names in the bible didn't help. Above my dad's name, "Rachel Lynn Hilson" was recorded. There had been another sister between my dad and Rose. I didn't know what happened to her, only that there had been some sort of accident when she was five. I didn't need any more details to know that the death of a five-year-old was something I didn't want to hear about. She was the reason people suggested that my new home was haunted.

I closed the bible and shoved it next to me on the bed. Then I returned my attention to the drawer it came from. There were several newspaper clippings, including an obituary for my grandma. I couldn't figure out why anyone would save some of the other clippings. There were some loose photographs. I recognized myself as a little girl in a few of them. In one I looked about three or four and I was sitting across a chess board from an older boy. I had no idea who he was and there were no names on the back. There was a date and it seemed to confirm that the little girl was me. I would have been four.

The next thing I pulled out was a book with a cloth cover of blue plaid. I held it for a few moments and fingered the cover. It was a journal and I was nervous about opening it.

Along with my aunt's will had been a hand written letter. It explained that I was the obvious choice since she had no children and her only brother had only one child. But then she went on to say that

19

she also wanted me to have everything because of a rare kinship between us. She felt that I was very much like her. She said she noticed it even when I was little. In the note, the word everything had been underlined twice. That felt like permission to read the journal, but I still wasn't sure it would be a good idea.

I opened it slowly to a random page in the middle. "Bananas, oatmeal, flour..." It was a grocery list. The next page was an actual journal entry. It talked about how many tomatoes she had picked that day and which of her neighbors might like to have some. It filled a whole page. I read several more pages and they were all mostly about gardening. After a half hour or so, I concluded that I had read enough and that gardening was not going to be my hobby.

As I closed the book though, I realized that there was a stack of letters tucked inside the front cover. They were all addressed to Rose and were from the same person. The return address was on her street, now my street. I flipped through the postmarks. There were three letters from about thirteen years earlier and a few more recent ones. I pulled out the oldest letter first and unfolded it.

> *My Flower,*
> *You must know by now that the kindness you have shown since Martha's passing has begun to rekindle something in me. Our visits are the highlight of my days. Your eyes used to tell me more than you would say. And what I see now gives me reason to hope you feel something for me as well. I must tell you that if we continue to spend time together I will be completely under your control. I tell you this not to request anything in return. Though it may be too late, if the thought of my devotion is in any way unpleasant to you, you should guard against it now.*
> *A L*
>
> *P.S. Please be careful with those fresh cinnamon rolls. They would win over much stronger men than I.*

The love letter was a lost art form. The most romantic note I ever got from Jacob was a text message that said, "I have never missed you more than I do right now." It was Thanksgiving. I was in the kitchen watching my mom prepare the meal and he was stuck in the next room with my dad.

Andrew was not the first person to say that I resembled Rose physically. Older pictures of her – there was one on the wall in my dining room as a matter of fact – proved how much we looked alike. Until that note in the will, I had never heard a comment about a personality match. Now though, after Jacob, I wondered how much I was like her. Other than a few priests, Rose was always the oldest person I knew who had never married. I still couldn't explain why I hadn't wanted to marry Jacob. I somehow knew it wasn't the right thing to do. Maybe I wasn't meant to marry anyone. Maybe God had a solitary life in mind for me like my aunt.

Yet Aunt Rose's life hadn't been completely solitary. These letters showed there had been some romance, which made it even stranger to me that she hadn't ended up with Al. He had obviously kept writing and still not won her over. I looked at the return address as I considered reading the next letter. I wondered if I ran by his house in the mornings. But when I thought about it, I realized the numbers went in the other direction. That's when it hit me. The letters weren't from Al. They were from A.L. Andrew Lately.

I felt awful for finding the letters and worse for reading one. Rose had possibly given me permission to invade her privacy, but Andrew had not. I carefully tucked all the letters back where I found them and continued digging through the drawer.

Chapter 5

I stopped kneeling by the bed when I was about twelve or thirteen. After that I said my prayers lying on the bed staring at the ceiling. It felt more like a conversation that way. When I was done, I closed my eyes and tried to think of what I might need to buy at the store the next day. It would be Saturday and I didn't run on Sunday so I had to think two days ahead. A box of crackers maybe and some carrots would be nice. I'd been eating a lot of raw foods lately. That wasn't necessarily part of the health kick. It had more to do with the not wanting to wash dishes kick. I'd been on that one for 25 years.

In the morning, I laced up my shoes as usual. It was extra humid, but I still kept up a good pace. I walked through the cool store long enough that I was no longer dripping and then took my things to Mabel.

"Morning, hon," she greeted me.

"Hello. How are you today?"

"Right as rain, which I hear we might get later."

"Might be nice. It's kind of sticky out there."

Mabel nodded. "You haven't had any more visits from your ghost, have you?"

"None."

"What about visits from a certain young officer of the law?"

I shook my head and diverted. "Oh, Mabel, there was something I was going to ask you."

"Ask away, hon."

"I'm hoping to find someone who can mow my lawn for me, like on a regular basis. Do you know anyone who does that?"

Mabel's eyes lit up. "You have definitely come to the right place," she said. "My oldest grandson is trying to earn some money mowing lawns this summer. Aiden just got out of school last week so he only has one client, other than me of course, so I know he'd love to do it for you. He's only fourteen, but he's becoming a real responsible young man."

"Fourteen? Would he need a ride to my place?"

"His dad could drop him off and pick him up if he needs a mower. He has a truck."

"I have a mower he can use. Provided he doesn't need me to show him how. If I knew that, I wouldn't need to hire someone."

"No shame in that, hon," Mabel said as she puffed herself up a bit. "I've never mowed grass in my life. That's what husbands are for. And sons and grandsons."

"Well, I guess I might have to borrow your grandson then."

"You leave the arrangements to me. What day of the week is good for you?"

I shrugged.

"Okay, I'll work it out and let you know."

"Thanks, Mabel."

I skipped "Things to Do" and started for home. I got there about 10 o'clock, which gave me time for a shower. I braided my hair while it was still wet. Instead of shorts, I grabbed a pretty blue sundress from my closet. Then I opened the door at the bottom of the stairs and sat down with a book. I gave up about 11 o'clock and relocked the door. Soon I was glad there was no one out walking as the sky darkened and thunder rumbled in the distance.

The rain pounded on my house and rattled the windows. The lights went out. It was very dark for midday. I thought I should hunt for flashlights or candles in case the power stayed off. I remembered seeing a box of tapers in the hutch in the dining room. I found three pairs of holders as well and a box of matches. The box felt very light. When I opened it, there were only two matches inside. I set the candles up on the kitchen table and began searching kitchen drawers for more matches. I wasn't even sure I'd need them, but the storm had me on edge and I felt better doing something.

Then I remembered the old matchbook in the upstairs nightstand. I checked the side door as I went up to make sure it was still locked. I knew that would be a habit as long as the key was out of my possession and maybe longer. House-shaking thunder roared as I made my way up the steps. It rattled my nerves and I wanted to get back downstairs. Right as I reached the doorway to the first bedroom, lightning lit the room for a split second and in that instant I clearly saw a person in there looking right at me. My heart froze in my chest and I choked on a scream.

More lightning showed that the person was me, my reflection in the mirror. I looked away from my own wild eyes and grabbed what I

23

had come for so fast I almost closed my fingers in the drawer. I ran down the stairs and as I was locking the door I remembered how I had had to enter the room to see myself the last time and I hadn't moved the mirror. I hadn't even touched it.

I went into the kitchen and lit one of the candles, hoping to warm the shiver from my spine. I planned to save most of them for real darkness, if necessary, but my hands were shaking so badly that I lit a second one. I felt a bit better with some light. I found some lunch and food helped, too.

Before long, the rain was reduced to a trickle. The clouds stayed though, leaving me in partial darkness all afternoon. I stayed in the kitchen and read a book by candlelight. I chose a comedy and smiling eased my nerves like nothing else. I thought about that mirror when I was calmer and convinced myself that I hadn't moved *that* far into the room to see myself the first time. I probably could have seen a bit of my reflection from the hallway and it was just the storm that told me otherwise.

Once I talked myself down, the power outage was merely an inconvenience. I ate my dinner by candlelight as well and started to wonder if the power would ever come back on. A loud noise made me jump before I realized that it was someone knocking on my front door. Then it was a wonderful sound. Sitting around waiting for the lights to turn on was kind of boring.

I moved the curtains a bit to peek out. The young man standing on my porch was not familiar to me. He wasn't holding a clipboard, but I might have opened the door to a salesman anyway. I was that bored and that lonely.

"Hello," I said as I felt the cooler outside air on my face. "Can I help you?"

"I, um…" The man swallowed hard. He seemed somehow surprised by me. Did he not expect an answer when he knocked? "I actually wondered if I could help you."

Ah, maybe he was a salesman. I waited for him to start his pitch.

"I saw the candles through the window as I drove by," he said.

"Yeah, my power is out," I told him.

He nodded. "That's what I thought and I, well, I noticed that everyone else on the street seems to have lights and I wondered if you needed any help. Have you already called the power company or do you need someone to call for you?"

"Oh!" Embarrassment slapped me in the face. This was one of those things that a grownup would know. Power didn't just magically come back on. You needed to ask someone to turn it on. "I guess I didn't think of that."

"I have the number right here." He pulled his phone out. "Do you want me to give it to you or should I call or... maybe both?" He smiled uncertainly and it made my eyes travel down to his left hand. That was not something I was in the habit of checking. I must have been very lonely.

"Do you want to come in for a minute?" I asked, and not because I had noticed the absence of a wedding ring. It seemed this might take a minute and it was getting awkward standing there with the door open.

"Sure," he said. He stepped past me and let me close the door behind him. "The address here is eleven sixteen, right?"

"Yes."

"Okay, why don't I go ahead and call while you find something to take the number in case you need it again later."

I nodded and said, "You can move into the kitchen where there's some light."

He also nodded and took a few steps towards the candles.

I pulled my phone out of my bag and stood next to him. He was obviously talking to a computer, one with several levels of menu. He kept his eyes on the floor while he talked and looked at me as he hung up. "They estimate it'll be about an hour. You ready for the number?"

He read it out to me when I nodded, then he said, "I'm Charlie, by the way. Charlie Tate."

"Rebecca Hilson," I answered.

"I knew your aunt. Not well, but she always seemed very nice. I was sorry to hear when she passed."

"Thank you. Everyone in town has been telling me what a nice lady she was. It helps me feel welcome."

"That's good. When I heard Rose Hilson's niece had moved into her house I was... I pictured someone quite a bit older."

"Yeah, my parents had me kind of late and Rose was older than my dad. Others have been surprised by the gap, too."

"Well, um, do you think you'll be okay until your power comes back? I can leave you my number, too, in case you need anything."

"No, you don't have to do that. Thanks though. I'm sure I'll be fine."

25

"If something does come up, I'm staying just three houses that way." He pointed the same way Andrew had pointed. That seemed to be a good direction. Maybe I'd have to run that way sometime. He was staying that way though, not living. I told myself I was disappointed at the temporary verb because he seemed so nice, not because I also thought he was nice-looking.

I nodded at him. "I'll keep that in mind. It'd be kind of sad if I couldn't survive an hour of darkness though."

Charlie made his way back to the front door. I followed and said, "Thanks for your help. I'm glad you came to check on me."

"Me, too. Have a good night."

I closed the door behind him and covertly watched through the window as he jumped into a black car in my driveway. His face was lit up by the interior light and he was wearing a wide grin.

I lit two more candles once I knew I probably wouldn't need to save them. Then I went back to my book. I was interrupted some time later by another knock. Maybe Charlie didn't believe I could survive an hour of darkness. I would have to let him know how I felt about him thinking that as soon as I finished being happy to see him again. When I glanced out the window though, I saw someone in a police uniform. Uh-oh. I opened the door quickly.

It was the same younger officer who had recently come to my aid. "Can I help you?" I asked a little nervously.

"Good evening, ma'am. We're just out checking for damage or problems after the storm. It looked as though your power is out and I wanted to make sure you're okay."

"Yeah, it's fine. I already called the power company and they said it should be back on shortly so..." I was interrupted by light and something beeping as the power was restored behind me. "There it is now," I said.

"You're all set then, I guess." He almost sounded disappointed.

"Yeah, thanks for checking though."

He nodded as I closed the door. I turned on the porch light for him because now I could.

Chapter 6

Some of my aunt's old clothes were in a pile on her lawn. I did not plan to put them there. I got ready for church early so I could stop at the thrift store on the way. When I took the first bag to my car, however, the seam split and dumped its contents on the grass. I stood over the pile and grumbled to myself something about cheap garbage bags. I wondered how to avoid the rest of them breaking on me. And I wondered how much time I could spend on this project before I was late for church.

I sighed and went into the house for another bag. The grass was still a bit squishy so putting my bare knees in it was not pleasant. My pink skirt was brushing the grass and I hoped that it, at least, was staying clean. I knelt there and began stuffing the clothes into the new bag. I didn't bother to refold anything that had come undone. I heard a male voice call out, "Hey, do you need a hand?"

There were two men walking up my driveway and I recognized both of them. It was Andrew Lately and Charlie Tate. Charlie didn't wait for an answer. He jogged the last half of the driveway and squatted next to me to help with the clothes.

"Thanks. The other bag broke open," I said in an attempt to explain why I had dumped clothes in the wet grass.

"Where are you headed with these?" he asked.

"My car." I nodded to the open trunk.

He lifted the bag as soon as it was full. "I think if I hold it on the bottom it'll stay together."

I turned to Andrew while Charlie carried the bag to my trunk.

"Nice to see you again, Andrew."

"Rose?"

"Rebecca," I said. "I'm her niece, remember?"

He nodded. Something wasn't right though. I couldn't tell if he had forgotten my name or meeting me altogether.

Charlie returned to us. "Have you met my grandfather?"

"Yeah, just a few days ago."

27

"Um, I didn't know if I should close the trunk," Charlie said. "Do you have anything else to put in there?"

"Seven more bags actually. Aunt Rose had a lot of clothes."

"Let me help you," he said.

"Oh, no. I've already interrupted your walk. I'll manage fine by myself."

Andrew folded his arms. "Nonsense. How could we walk off knowing there's a lady in need. You let my boy help you."

"Well…" I wanted to insist, but had a feeling that wouldn't do any good. Andrew looked determined to wait and Charlie looked keen on helping. "Come on." I motioned for Charlie to follow me into the house. I took him to the dining room where the pile of bags was obvious. We each picked up one – by the bottom, not the handle.

Charlie said, "I hope your power came back pretty quickly last night."

"It was probably only twenty minutes after you left."

He followed me to the car quietly. We noticed Andrew had taken a seat on the bench near what used to be a fabulous garden. Now it was just a patch of yard that was more weeds than grass. Charlie made another attempt at conversation as we walked back to the house. "So," he said, "these were your late aunt's things?"

"Yeah, and it might not even be all her clothes. There's a bunch of stuff upstairs I haven't looked through. I cannot believe how many boxes are up there."

"Has no one… I'm sorry if I'm prying, but I'm surprised no one had gone through her stuff before. Hasn't she been gone a year or so?"

"Almost," I said. "My dad was here a few times right after she died. He tried to take care of anything immediate. He had the power and water shut off and cleared out the fridge and cupboards so there'd be nothing to spoil. Everything else has been just sort of waiting for me. I think I'm going to be cleaning it out for months."

"Sounds like you might need more help than just these bags," Charlie said as he dropped one into the trunk on top of mine.

"Honestly, the hardest part has been figuring out where to start and I'm not sure anyone can help me with that."

"I can see that kind of project being overwhelming. I'll get the rest by myself. Why don't you wait with Grandpa?"

"Okay, thanks." I walked over and stood in front of Andrew. He was staring at the sad rectangle in my yard. I stared at it, too, trying to picture it the way it used to look.

"It's cooler after the storm," he mumbled.

He was right. The rain had washed the humidity out of the air and left a satisfying warmth without the oppressive heat.

"Rose loved this garden." Andrew seemed to shake off sadness as he forced himself to look up at me. "Did we get your car loaded?"

I looked over my shoulder and saw Charlie putting the last bag into my trunk. He had to squash things down to make it all fit. I said, "That's the last of it."

Andrew gripped the armrest of the wrought iron bench and pushed himself to standing. We took a few steps towards the driveway and Charlie met us halfway.

"Thanks again," I said to both of them. "It was much easier with help."

"You're welcome," Charlie said simply and he turned to leave.

Andrew stopped him. "Hold your horses, son. I think we should invite this pretty young lady over to help you babysit this afternoon."

Charlie rolled his eyes and muttered something about not being anyone's babysitter while his grandfather turned to me. "Do you have plans for the afternoon, Miss?"

I planned to spend the afternoon wandering around the house looking for something productive to do. That was how I spent most of my afternoons. "I'm not doing anything special," I told Andrew.

"In that case, we would be delighted if you would give us the pleasure of your company for a few hours."

I glanced at Charlie to see if he was on board with the invitation. He looked hopeful so I asked what time.

"2 o'clock," Andrew said definitively.

"Okay. Which house is it?"

"The third one that way," Charlie pointed away from town. "It has a red door."

"So we can expect you?" Andrew asked.

I told them I'd be there and watched them walk away. Charlie looked back once and smiled at me. I was already looking forward to the afternoon as I drove to the thrift store. It was closed on Sundays.

Now I would be early to church. This was a potential problem because my parents were usually early and I was still trying to avoid them without being too obvious that I was avoiding them. My parents lived in the city, only a few blocks from our church. Port Harris wasn't exactly a city. It was a much larger town than Hartford though and had things the smaller town did not, like movie theaters, chain restaurants and thrift stores that were closed on Sundays. People in Hartford said they were going to "the city" when they needed one of those things.

Port Harris was about a 30-minute drive to the west, which was not terribly inconvenient unless you were headed that way as the sun was going down. I pulled into the church parking lot and noticed my parents' car. I sat in mine after I parked and decided to play with my phone for a minute. I had voicemail. It was my mom.

"Hi, honey. We just wanted to check in and make sure you survived yesterday's storm. A lot of people had their power knocked out. And some branches came down. Let us know if you need anything. We hope to see you in church later. We love you. Bye."

I waited until the last minute and then went in and sat in the back pew. My dad saw me as people were standing up to leave. I smiled and waved at him as though everything was fine. Then I hurried to my car before he and my mom could get through all the people between us.

I stopped at a drive-through on my way home and got two salads, one for lunch and one to eat later in the week. Despite what my parents might think, I did plan for my future. By 1 o'clock, the only thing I was doing was waiting for 2 o'clock. It might have looked as though I was reading a book, but I was checking the time after nearly every paragraph. Finally, I could start the short walk. I wasn't sure which of the guys I was more excited to see. Andrew was easy to talk to. There wasn't enough talking in my solitary life. And Charlie seemed interested in me, which I found interesting.

This far from the center of Hartford, the houses were spread out enough that the third house was at least a quarter of a mile. The red door had two vertical rows of diamond-shaped windows down the front. I knocked between them. The red door swung open and Charlie appeared behind it.

"Hi, Rebecca," he said. "Come on in."

He led me into a smallish living room that was covered in doilies. There was one under each of the three lamps on end tables, several overlapping ones on the coffee table, and one draped over the back of each of the two matching stuffed chairs. Andrew was in one of those chairs and he rose to greet me, though I tried to tell him it wasn't necessary.

"You look so much like your aunt," he said as we all sat down. "Except, if I wasn't betraying her memory, I'd say that you were a hair lovelier. Isn't she beautiful, Charlie?" Andrew looked at his grandson, who nodded without looking at me. I thought we needed a new topic.

"Have you lived in this house a long time?" I asked.

"A very long time," Andrew answered. "Martha and I bought this place soon after we married. Let's see, we married in '59 so it must have been '60 or '61 when we moved here." Andrew went on for quite a while about the house, describing what it looked like when they moved in and various things they'd done to it since then.

When he took a break, Charlie asked if I had plans for Rose's house.

"I'm still trying to figure that out," I said. "I'm living in this house that's full of someone else's things, which makes me feel like a guest. I'd like to make the house feel like my house, but because I feel like a guest, I feel like I don't have the right to move things around or get rid of them. I haven't changed anything outside the bedroom yet."

Charlie nodded sympathetically and Andrew said, "Well, dear, it sounds like you need to approach your situation like everything else in life – one step at a time."

"But how do I even know where to start?"

"You start with what's in front of you. Take each item and ask yourself two questions. Do I need this and do I want this. If the answer to both questions is no, then you get rid of it. Hopefully by finding someone else who needs or wants it.

"What if the answer to *do I want this* is always *I don't know?*"

Andrew gave me a shrewd smile. "We always know what we want, dear. We just have a lot of reasons for telling ourselves that we should or shouldn't want something and those shoulds get in the way."

I didn't mean to argue with him, but I knew I looked skeptical and that he could tell I was skeptical.

"Take me," he went on, "right now I want a glass of water and I want Charlie here to fetch it for me. But I know I shouldn't want his help because it still stings that the family thinks I need him here to look after me. So I'm sitting here trying to convince myself that I don't really want that glass of water."

Charlie laughed and stood up. "All right, Grandpa, I can take a hint. Rebecca, can I get you something while I'm up?"

I smiled at Andrew. "I guess I want a glass of water, too." Then I looked at Charlie and added, "Please?"

"Be right back," he said.

As soon as Charlie was out of the room, Andrew leaned in a bit and asked, "Are you and my Charlie an item?"

"I, uh, I just met Charlie yesterday."

"You're not already spoken for, are you?"

I shook my head. Honesty was usually simple. It still made my face a bit warm.

Andrew leaned back in his chair. "Charlie will be glad to hear that. You should stay for dinner."

It seemed a little early to commit to dinner and that didn't sound like an official invitation so I just said, "We'll see."

"Fair enough, uh, what did Charlie just call you?"

"Rebecca."

"Have you told me that before?"

"Yes."

"I'll try to remember this time. Otherwise people are going to start calling me Forgetful Lately, right?"

I smiled at the joke that was somehow more *and* less amusing the second time. Charlie came back with three glasses. He put one on the coffee table in front of me and by the look on his face I thought he might have heard the Forgetful Lately joke more than twice. Then he handed a glass to Andrew.

As Charlie sat down with the remaining glass, Andrew took a small sip from his and then put it down as he said, "Well, I can hardly keep my eyes open. I think I'll go lie down for a bit."

Charlie tried to help his grandfather up, but the older man shook him off. "You just convince our guest to stay for dinner while I'm gone," he said. Andrew winked at me as he left the room. I wondered if the water had only been a scheme to get Charlie out of the room for a minute.

Chapter 7

With Andrew off for a nap, Charlie and I sat looking at each other a bit awkwardly. I sipped at my water and finally asked, "How long are you staying with your grandfather?"

"As long as he'll let me, but only on weekends."

"I don't understand."

"Yeah, it's a bit complicated." Charlie sucked in some air and then I guess decided to continue with an explanation. "We've been worried about Grandpa. He's been having memory problems for maybe a year now. Then about a month ago, he passed out while he was at the market. The EMTs were called and it appeared that he had messed up his medications... possibly taken something twice because he forgot he had already taken it. It ended up not being too serious, but it kind of scared us all. So my mom convinced him – he's her dad – to move in with her and my dad. That didn't exactly work out." Charlie stopped and chuckled to himself. "Let's just say," he continued, "that the three of them drove each other nuts in such close quarters. Grandpa really wanted to come home. So we had a big family meeting. My mom and dad and my sisters and cousins and even my aunt who lives in Maryland was there via Skype. I'm not going to tell you some of the crazy ideas people came up with.

"In the end, it was decided that I would come and spend my weekends here. I live in Port Harris so it's not a big deal to drive over here on Fridays. I'll head back to my apartment some time after dinner. My mom and my aunt are taking turns stopping by on weekday mornings. Anyway, Grandpa moved back home on, um, Wednesday and this is my first shift of probably many."

"It's very kind of you to sacrifice your weekends to help your family."

Charlie shook his head. "Don't think I'm some kind of saint. I don't do anything on the weekends so there wasn't really anything to sacrifice. In fact, *this* is the most enjoyable weekend I've had in a very long time."

"I'm glad your grandpa is keeping you entertained."

"He's not the only one." Charlie looked away as he said it and seemed a bit embarrassed. As he pretended to straighten the doily on the table next to him, I pretended I was focused on taking a drink while I studied his appearance. He was wearing khaki pants and a sky blue polo shirt. His shoulders filled out the shirt more than adequately. He had slightly shaggy hair a few shades darker than mine and was more cute than handsome. What struck me the most, and I had noticed it the first time I met him, was a dimple on his left cheek. It was the only horizontal dimple I had ever seen and it made his smile memorable.

Charlie turned back to me somewhat suddenly. "Oh, I saw you this morning," he said.

"I know. And I thanked you for your help."

"No, I mean later. I saw you at church. We go to the same one. I tried to say hi, but it looked like you were in a hurry to get out of there."

"Oh, I'm sorry, I didn't see you." Now it was my turn to be embarrassed. He had caught me running away from my parents, not that he knew that. When I looked back at Charlie he cast his eyes down. I got the impression that he had been studying me, too. I impulsively decided that if we were going to study each other, we might as well do it openly.

"How old are you?" I asked.

"29," he said. I would not have guessed he was older than me.

"Have you ever been married?"

He looked either surprised or worried as he slowly shook his head.

"Do you have a favorite food?"

"I don't know about a favorite, but I do really like anything grilled. I can't really do that at my place. There's a common area where you're allowed to grill, but I don't see myself dragging my dinner across the complex. Anyway, I've been looking forward to using my grandpa's grill. We're having hamburgers for dinner if that helps convince you to stay." His brow went up in a question.

I hadn't had a hamburger in months. It sounded delicious. "It might help," I said. "Now you ask me something."

"Um, okay… how old are you?"

"25."

"Have *you* ever been married?"

"No."

"Ever been close?"

34

"Close?"

"Close to getting married. That just... I wondered what made that the first thing you asked."

"It was the second," I clarified. I knew what he meant though. It had been a bit abrupt. "But no, I haven't. Someone asked me, but I wasn't close to saying yes so I guess I wasn't close to getting married. I think it only came to mind because I've been thinking about my aunt so much lately and she never got married. It makes me wonder if... people say I'm like her."

"Okay..." Charlie looked thoughtful for a moment before he added, "Where did you live before you came to her house?"

"We lived in Hartford when I was really little, then my dad got a job in Atlanta and we were there for just two years. Then we came back, sort of, and lived in Port Harris when I was nine. The house they bought then is the one they still live in and I lived with them until a few weeks ago because I was still in school."

"Yeah? What were you studying?"

"I got a degree in accounting and then an MBA."

"What are you going to do with that?"

I shrugged.

"You didn't have a job in mind?" he asked.

"I'll need to find something eventually. But honestly, I just sort of took classes that I seemed to be good at. My only goal was graduating. Now I'm thinking about trying another degree. But I can't seem to decide and really I'm just kind of sick of school. My parents *suggested* that I might be able to 'find myself' if I spent some time alone. So here I am alone. Do you have a geographical history?"

"Geographical history? You mean like a bare bones life story?"

"I guess that's what I mean."

"Well, I grew up here in Hartford, near downtown. My parents moved to the city when I was seventeen and since I had just started my last year of high school, they let me stay with my grandpa so I could graduate with my class. Then I moved back in with them for college and law school. That was kind of a long commute, but I usually had recorded lectures or something to listen to so I could study and drive."

"Oh, so you're a lawyer?"

"Um, no. I only did one year of law school. It seemed like a good idea when I started, but then all I could think about was how much money it was costing and that it was really, really boring. So I quit and got a nice office job that is also kind of boring. But the money is flowing the right way now, I work with good people and it's very 9-to-5 so I have plenty of free time to spend with my grandfather and his neighbors."

Charlie's smile gave me the impression that he was very glad we had met. I thought I should dial it back and not seem quite so eager to know him. I was really only looking for friends at the moment. "How long do you think your grandfather will be sleeping?"

"I'm not sure. I think it was only twenty minutes or so yesterday. Actually though… I should warn you about something." He exhaled slowly. "He might be, um… confused when he wakes up. Most of the time, Grandpa is pretty lucid. Even though he's forgetful it's like he knows when he's forgetting something so it doesn't seem so bad. But he tends to wake up confused. First thing in the morning and after a nap, it's as if his brain takes longer to wake up than the rest of him. Yesterday he kept asking where my grandmother was and she's been dead for fifteen years. It was kind of unsettling."

"Sounds like it."

"Anyway, I don't want you to feel bad if he's surprised that we have company or something."

"Do you think it'd be better if I left?"

"No, please don't," Charlie said. "Even if he doesn't immediately remember it, he was sincere in his dinner invitation and I think we should respect that. And, well, *I* want you to stay."

I nodded and said something about how much I enjoyed Andrew's stories. Charlie offered to give me a tour of the house. We moved into a formal dining room. It had a large windowed cabinet full of fine china and crystal glassware. Charlie pointed to a landscape painting. "One of my cousins painted this. She's very talented and we've tried to talk her into selling her work, but she insists it's just a hobby." Instead of appreciating the talent, I found myself a little jealous of it. I had already ruled out painting as my passion.

He took me into the kitchen where we found Andrew staring at the coffee pot. He seemed to be trying to figure out how to use it. Charlie gently reminded him that it wasn't morning and that he didn't like to drink coffee in the afternoon because it kept him awake at night. Andrew thought I was Rose again. When I said my name though, something seemed to click. He looked between me and Charlie and gradually came around.

I did stay for dinner. I enjoyed watching Charlie man the grill and Andrew did most of the talking while we ate. He concentrated on stories of his kids when they were young. Charlie seemed to particularly like the ones about his mom, even the ones he had heard before.

The hamburger was one of the best I'd ever tasted. I insisted on leaving as soon as I was done. I hoped if I didn't overstay my welcome, they'd be more likely to invite me back. Andrew thanked me for coming and told Charlie to walk me home.

When we stepped outside, I said, "You really don't have to walk with me. It's not far."

"No, I do. You heard what he said."

"Okay, I guess I wouldn't want to get you in trouble."

As we walked home, he told me the name of the woman who lived in the first house and about the couple in the house closer to mine, a Mr. and Mrs. Riser. Their son had been one of Charlie's good friends as a kid. He moved away after high school and Charlie hadn't managed to stay in touch with him, but he sometimes got updates from the parents. At my driveway, he started talking about the next weekend.

"I'll be back on Friday in time to have dinner with Grandpa. Do you think I could give you a call after that and see what your weekend looks like? Maybe there'll be a time we can get together again."

"I already know what my weekend looks like. It looks like me surrounded by a bunch of stuff I need to organize and don't know how. Some of it is kind of heavy though. How do you feel about manual labor as entertainment?"

"I think under the right circumstances, it could be very entertaining."

"In that case, I'll give you my number and then spend the week making a list of things I want you to move for me."

Charlie said, "Perfect."

Chapter 8

An ice pack seemed like a good idea on Monday. Yogurt was on my short shopping list and some days I walked home more slowly than others. I wrapped it in a dish towel so it wouldn't make a puddle on the bottom of my backpack. Mabel looked happy to see me.

"Hi, hon. Hear your lights went out with the storm."

"Yeah, only for a few hours. I survived."

"Aiden's got you penciled in for this afternoon, if that's okay with you."

I had to think back to our last conversation. Aiden was the grandson who mowed lawns. "Okay."

"He was gonna do mine today, but I told him your place was getting to be a jungle so mine could wait 'til tomorrow. He'll come by right after lunch."

"Great. How much does he charge?"

"$30."

I nodded. "Thanks for setting it up." I went to the bank next to use the ATM. I didn't usually carry much cash, but I figured the odds were against a 14-year-old accepting credit cards. Then I made my way over to "Things to Do" not feeling any more excited about clay than I had a few days ago.

The door announced my entrance with no shortage of jingling. Jill was rearranging a shelf near the front of the store. "I'll be right… Hey, Rebecca." She stood up and gave me her full attention. "How is clay feeling now?" she asked.

I winced, even though I knew that would be the first thing she asked. "I'm sorry," I said. "It's just not growing on me."

"That's okay, it doesn't hurt to rule things out. But I'm afraid this means I'm going to have to give you homework."

"Homework?"

She put both hands on her hips and gave me a serious look. "I think it will help," she insisted.

"What kind of homework?"

"I want you to spend a few days making a list of things you like. Foods or colors or clothes… anything. Just any time you think to yourself, 'I like this,' put that thing on the list."

"Really?"

"Once you get up to… let's say 20 things, bring the list back to me for inspiration."

This was the first time I considered that perhaps my future passion was in the hands of a lunatic. But she was a likable lunatic so I intended to at least attempt this homework. It didn't sound difficult. Strange yes, but not difficult. I assured her I would give it a try as the door released another round of tintinnabulation.

Jill said, "Hi, Jack."

The guy who entered must be her husband. I hadn't met Jack yet. He was, somehow, pretty much what I expected. Their names were the only things cute about Jack and Jill. They both appeared to be in their early thirties. Jill's straight bob was dyed the blackest black with light pink highlights. Her right ear was pierced all the way around and I had not yet seen her without a pair of crazy knee socks. Jack sort of completed the set. His very blond hair was cut so short he almost looked bald. He was slightly shorter than Jill and where he was standing at the moment made my mind start trying to figure out which size knitting needles would fit through the holes in his earlobes.

"I had a delivery next door so I thought I'd stop in and say hi to our future child." Jack patted his wife's belly and said, "Please be a boy. Please be a boy." Then he gave her a quick one-armed hug. "And hi to you, too."

"Jack, this is Rebecca." Jill waved her hand between us. "Rebecca, Jack."

"Hey, nice to meet you," he said. "Jill has been so excited about having a new patient."

"She's definitely been patient with me anyway."

Jill wagged a finger at me. "We're going to figure you out," she said.

Jack said, "Well, I won't interrupt." He waved to both of us and went back out the door.

I looked at Jill. "He wants a boy, huh?"

She laughed. "He thinks he does because he's worried he doesn't know anything about girls. But he would totally dote on a daughter so I'm not worried."

"Are you gonna find out soon?"

39

"I'm not sure. The ultrasound is scheduled for next Wednesday, but I want to be surprised and Jack wants to know. We're trying to come to an agreement before then."

"You don't think he could keep it a secret from you?"

She snorted and gave me a look that said I'd sooner start sculpting clay. Then I told her I'd better get home and start working on my list. She wished me luck.

I took my time walking home and I took my time in the shower. I took my time picking out a simple pair of shorts and a tank top that would be comfortable for working in my stuffy house. I had a lot of work to do in the house. It was nearly lunch time though. I didn't really have time for a project. Instead I browsed the web to make sure there had been no major developments in the world while I was living under my house-shaped rock. I wasn't sure my typical source of news reached outside Hartford.

After lunch I remembered that I was expecting my new yard service any time. I wouldn't want it to look as though he was interrupting something.

A few neighbors had stopped by to introduce themselves when I first moved in and of course I had two visitors checking on my power situation. Aiden was the first person to ring my doorbell. Fourteen sounded like a kid so I was surprised to open the door and find someone taller than me. I'm 5'6" and he couldn't have been more than two or three inches taller, but I was still surprised because I was expecting shorter. He was very skinny and wore dark rimmed glasses.

"Hi," he said. "I'm Aiden Thorpe. My grandmother said you'd be expecting me."

"Yes, she told me you could help me take care of my jungle."

"It is kind of tall. I hope your mower can handle it."

"Oh, are you going to use mine?"

Aiden turned a bit red. "Grandma said that was okay. I have to get my dad to drive me if I bring a mower, but I walked." He held up a red plastic container. "I brought gas if we need it."

This kid clearly knew more about mowing lawns than I did. "Yeah, if my mower works for you then that works for me. Your grandma said you had one so I... anyway, come on," I motioned him to follow me. "It's faster if we go through the house."

He followed me out the back door and to the garage behind the house. "It's right over here."

40

"Sweet!" he exclaimed. "This is way better than ours."

Since I had no idea what made one mower better than another, I simply nodded. "So you're all set then?"

"Um, do you have any special instructions for me?"

"Like what?" I asked. If he was about to ask me how I wanted it cut the only thing I'd be able to say would be shorter.

"I mean do you have a garden or any plants I need to be careful around. I nipped my grandmother's flowers last year. She didn't take it well."

"Oh, no. Anything the mower can cut, just have at it."

"Okay, and, um…" He looked nervous again. "Well, if you pay me now I won't have to bother you again when I'm done."

"Right. That's a good system, not that it'd be a bother." I had exactly $30 in my pocket, which I handed over.

It took Aiden nearly two hours to mow my jungle back to a yard. I couldn't do any work inside the house while work was happening outside. I kept thinking Aiden might need me for something and I should be available just in case.

It was around 3 o'clock in the afternoon when there was no longer anything stopping me from getting to work. I went into the bedroom and stood there for a moment. It was a long moment. The bedroom had been an obvious place to start because I needed a place to put my clothes. Now my clothes were in the closet and I hadn't brought much else with me. I couldn't think of anything else that really needed to be done in that room except… that basket was kind of full. I should definitely do a load of laundry.

The washing machine was older than I was, possibly by many years. I didn't know if it might quit on me so I felt I should keep an eye on it while it was running. Watching a washing machine doesn't take a lot of concentration. I let my mind wander. First I thought about the fact that I had been home for several hours and had only been able to think of two things that I liked – blueberries and having someone else mow my lawn. I didn't think Jill would accept the second answer since it had more to do with me *not* liking mowing the lawn. I wasn't supposed to make a list of things I didn't like. That would have been easier.

I thought about the other list I was supposed to be making. I hadn't thought of a single thing I'd want Charlie to move for me. If I didn't have a few chores, he might think I just wanted to see him. Then I thought about the fact that I *did* want to see him.

41

The upstairs needed the most work. Perhaps I could find things up there that were heavy and things that I liked. And as I thought about it, I realized that I already had. I liked that mirror and I wanted to bring it downstairs. I could put that on both lists.

And then, possibly because I was thinking of the upstairs, I heard a sound from up there. In a quiet moment when the washer switched cycles, I heard what sounded like a scream. It wasn't one of those horror movie shrieks. It was softer, like the noise a child might make on a playground.

I sucked my breath in hard, but then I willed away the fear. I had already been scared twice by things that were not scary. It wasn't going to happen again. I marched myself to the stairs and let myself in. The outside door was locked. I stepped purposefully up the stairs repeating, "Just find the source. Just find the source. Just find the source."

I checked the bathroom. It seemed fine. I checked the first bedroom, slowly so as not to startle myself in the mirror. It also seemed fine. I checked the other two bedrooms. They were also just as I remembered. I stared intently at the attic door. Did I dare? I had to find the source. And then I noticed fresh bird poop on one of the windows. Of course. A bird could have made that sound. It had to have been a bird.

Chapter 9

I didn't stop at "Things to Do" on Tuesday because my list for Jill still only had two items on it. As soon as I cleaned up from the morning sweat fest, I went and stood in the dining room. All the way home I had been thinking about how little I had accomplished the day before. And by little I meant nothing. I had done nothing. Today I was going to do *something*. Now that the dining room table was no longer covered in garbage bags full of clothes – although they were still in the trunk of my car – I had no excuse not to work on this room. First I needed music. I put on something upbeat and looked around the room.

I concentrated on Andrew's advice. He had said to pick something in front of me and decide if I needed or wanted it. The first part was easy. The dining room table seated twelve. It jumped out as being in front of me. Did I need an enormous table? I didn't need one today. Beyond that I didn't know. What if I reconnected with some of my mom's family? I had met at least eleven people in town. What if I decided to host a dinner party? I asked myself instead if I wanted the huge table. Kind of. I mean, it was a pretty table with scrollwork on the legs and a shiny, nearly flawless surface. But it filled up the whole room. Maybe I wanted the space more.

I tried to find something else that was in front of me and found myself looking past everything in the room and out the window. There was a man standing in my front yard. He was fairly thin and tall but slightly stooped. His hair was also thin and a silvery gray. It was Andrew. He was standing there staring at my side yard, probably where the garden had been, with the saddest expression on his face.

There probably wasn't anything I could say that would make him feel better about me killing the garden. I thought I should say hello though. He startled slightly as I approached. Then he smiled at me and said, "I trust my Charlie was a gentleman when he walked you home the other night."

"Of course." I was slightly uneasy about the insinuation that there was something between me and Charlie but mostly relieved that Andrew knew who I was.

"Glad to hear it." His eyes went back to the weedy grass.

"I'm sorry the garden's not there anymore."

"It's probably for the best," he said. "The garden helps me remember that Rose is gone." He shook his head. "I've been on autopilot. The clock said 10:15 and I slipped on my shoes to come have tea with Rose. Every day but Sunday we had tea at 10:30. I looked forward to it so much. The habit was easy to keep and not easy to quit. Twelve years you know… I walked all the way over here before I remembered. The house looks different without a garden."

"Will you come in and sit for a bit? I'm afraid I don't have any tea, but I'd love some company."

"That's kind of you. Perhaps I will sit a spell."

He sat in the same chair as before. I wondered if that had been his spot for twelve years. "The inside of the house hasn't changed much," he commented.

I knew it wasn't a dig, but it felt like a judgment on my lack of progress. "I'm still trying to decide what to do with the place," I said. "Would you be upset if I made it look a lot different?"

He laughed. "Oh, honey, I've spent my whole life just accepting the changes around me. My Martha had new carpets put in the whole house while I was at work one day. Didn't say a word ahead of time or ask if I liked the color. I got home and she said, 'I got us new carpet today.' I said, 'I see that.' And you know what she said then?"

I shook my head.

"She said, 'See that you keep it clean.'"

Something about that story reminded me of my parents. I couldn't remember my mom doing anything quite so drastic. My dad had a habit though of saying "I like what you like" whenever Mom mentioned something around the house. That must have come from somewhere. "Well," I said, "carpets are beyond me right now. I need to get rid of a lot of stuff on top of the carpets before I can even think about the carpets."

"You'll get there. You have plenty of time."

Maybe time was my problem. Maybe if I had a deadline I could focus. At the moment I didn't even want to focus the conversation on the mess. "You mentioned William before," I said. "Is he your only sibling?"

"Yes. Mama used to say that she prayed for more babies but they never came."

"And is William still around?"

"Depends what you mean by around. He's still kickin' but he and his wife moved up to Michigan when his boys started giving them grandbabies. He had three boys and I had three girls. I have more grandchildren though. And a great-grandbaby." He listed all his grandchildren in order. Charlie was the oldest, but he couldn't remember the name of the youngest one. He told me some about William's family. Then he took out his wallet and showed me some pictures. One was much older than the rest. It showed him with his wife and their kids when the kids were still very small. He looked a little like Charlie in the picture. Enough of the pictures sparked stories that by the time he got through the stack, we had been talking for an hour.

"I best mosey, dear," Andrew said as he put the wallet back in his pocket. "It's nearly lunchtime and I don't want to intrude."

I considered inviting him to stay for lunch. I was going to eat a banana and munch on some crackers. That didn't seem like something you offered to company. I suggested something else instead. "Would you like to come back tomorrow?" I asked. "I'll even get tea."

"I don't want to trouble you."

"It's no trouble. Please come."

He smiled at me. I think he liked the idea and was only hesitating to be polite. "I accept then. Just promise me that if I forget to come, you won't take it as a snub. I don't know why some things stay with me and some don't." He rose to leave. "Speaking of which, what is your name again?"

"Rebecca."

"I'm sorry, Rebecca. I just think of Rose whenever I look at you and that seems to drive any other names right out of my head."

"No need to apologize. Rose is a pretty name. If that's the worst thing you ever call me, I think we'll get along just fine."

"I think we will, my dear." He reached up and gave my shoulder a slight squeeze. He took a few steps towards the stairs. The door to the upstairs was in the corner of the living room. I think it was when he realized it was closed that he turned around. "I should go out the front like I came in."

I shrugged. "Either way."

45

He pulled a set of keys out of his pocket. "Rose gave me this key for the side door. I should give that to you."

"No, I... I want you to keep it. I like that I'll know where to find a spare if I ever lock myself out." The key wouldn't do me much good if the inside door was locked. But that wasn't the real reason I insisted he keep it anyway. The key was the only thing my aunt hadn't left to me and I simply couldn't take the weight of one more thing.

He put the keys back. "You come to me any time you need it. Until tomorrow then."

I held the door open and watched him hold tightly to the railing as he made his way down the porch steps. Then he turned back and we both waved as I closed the door.

After my very simple lunch, I had an important project. It was something that couldn't be put off. I needed to learn how to make tea. I opened my laptop for research. Some articles talked about leaves and strainers, but if you used disposable tea bags all you needed to do was boil water. I could do that. But I still needed supplies. I went into the kitchen and started opening cabinets. I found a tray that would work for serving. I may not have ever made tea, but I had seen it done on TV. If TV was reliable in this case, tea was always served on a tray.

Aunt Rose had at least a half dozen teapots. One was metal with a wooden handle and had a flap on the spout that I guessed would whistle. The rest were ceramic with different patterns on the sides. It seemed that the metal one you put on the stove and the others could be used for serving. I picked the one I liked best – it had little strawberry plants on both sides – and washed it out. But then I couldn't find any cups or saucers that matched it. If the cups didn't match, I might as well pour from the metal pot.

My second favorite was pale blue with white chevrons. I looked for cups before I washed it. There was also a small sugar bowl with a tiny cute spoon. Would Andrew want sugar? Would I? I thought I better put sugar on my shopping list for tomorrow, too.

Once I had my tea set ready, I went back to the dining room. I didn't have any better ideas about what to do with the room than I had the other 37 times I had stood in the doorway. There was a thud that sounded as though it came from upstairs. I knew it must have been outside though, perhaps someone down the street slamming a car door. I thought about how I had let the bird scare me the day before. I had been so scared when I went to investigate, but I had done it

46

anyway. I could be brave enough to make at least one decision about this infernal dining room.

My gut told me that I liked the table. It also told me that it was probably larger than I would ever need. My eyes told me there were two leaves in the middle. I was very close to making a decision. The problem was that if I took out the leaves and the four chairs around them, they'd still be in the room. There were no closets in the house that would fit even one chair. I knew then what had to be done. I found that way overdue library book and drove to the city.

Chapter 10

Learning how to make tea was the easy part. I discovered that tea was not merely a drink, but a whole category of drinks. There must be thousands of varieties because even our small town grocery store had a whole section set aside for tea. Eventually I settled on some kind of sampler. Surely at least one of the eight flavors in the box would be something Andrew could swallow. At least for one day. If we made it a regular appointment, I'd find out what he liked.

"Hi, Mabel," I said at the front of the store.

"Rebecca Hilson! Have you been holding out on me?"

"Um, I don't think so." I had a feeling this accusation had to do with my supposed ghost. I was wrong.

"I hear you were out walking with Charlie Tate on Sunday. Why haven't you told me about this budding romance of yours?"

"Because there's nothing to tell."

"I don't know. Trudy said the two of you made a mighty cute couple."

Hartford's gossip mill was truly amazing. I had walked past two houses with a guy and now the whole town was planning our wedding. I thought it best to head this one off with a bit of reality. "I had dinner with Andrew Lately. Charlie was there and he walked me home to be neighborly. That's the whole story."

"I know Charlie's coming back every weekend for a while. You'll let me know if you see him again?"

"I'll try to keep you in the loop."

"I hope so, hon. I didn't appreciate coming late to the party this time. Everyone knows I see you every morning and I knew nothing."

"Okay, I'll see you tomorrow." I gathered my things and got out of there. Late to the party indeed. How many people had heard this story before it got to Mabel?

I had the downstairs door unlocked in case Andrew came in that way. It looked as though he started towards the side door and then turned back to the front. I thought that was a good sign that he would know who I was. I didn't count on him remembering my name

48

though. I put on the kettle as soon as he was seated and showed him the options. It's possible he was just being nice, but he said they all looked good before selecting a flavor. I took something else so as not to drink his favorite. I didn't know how any of them tasted anyway. When the kettle whistled, I jumped up as though I served tea all the time. Then I surreptitiously copied Andrew to make my own cup.

"Not bad for your first tea party," Andrew commented as he sipped his cup. I was letting mine cool off a bit. "This was always good with Rose's honey biscuits."

"Honey biscuits?" I said. "I think I saw that one."

"What's that, dear?"

"Oh, when I was looking for teapots I came across a big box of recipes. I wonder if you might be able to do me a favor."

"I'll certainly try."

"Well, I don't know if Rose cooked for you much or if you only had tea, but... to be honest, I don't know how to cook and was looking through the recipes trying to decide which ones might be good. Anyway, I thought if she had made some for you, you could offer some opinions."

"Everything Rose made was delicious. But I can especially attest to her baked goods being well worth attempting. The honey biscuits of course, blueberry scones... oh, and cinnamon rolls that you could smell baking clear down to my house. The heat will mar the table, dear. You'll want to keep that on the saucer."

I had just set my cup down directly on the coffee table. It hadn't occurred to me that the saucers served a purpose other than looking cute with the cups. I quickly moved it back to the saucer, but there was a dull circle where the cup had been.

"I'm sorry, dear. You can probably find someone to retouch that finish."

I shrugged. "I haven't decided if I'm keeping this table or not. I'll live with it for now."

Andrew looked at the table for a moment. "You know what? I think this one might be new. Yeah," he ran his hand around a corner, "Rose's table had sharper corners. I remember I caught my shin on one of those corners and was limping around the rest of the day."

"I wouldn't be surprised if the table you remember is upstairs. There's a whole bunch of furniture in one of the bedrooms up there. Actually, I was thinking of asking Charlie to help me move some of it on Saturday."

49

"My Charlie? Is he coming to see you?"

"He offered to help me out a bit while he's staying with you. You don't mind sharing him, do you?"

Andrew looked at me more seriously than I expected. He said, "You just be careful you don't go breaking his heart. He's a good boy. He doesn't deserve that."

I expected the answer even less than I had the serious look. It was time to move on. "I might ask him to help me go through some boxes instead. There's a whole bunch of random stuff up there and I don't even know what most of it is. Do you think he'd rather move furniture or open boxes?"

Andrew started smiling again. "Definitely the boxes. He's a bit of an explorer. Has he told you about his hobby yet?"

"No, I didn't know Charlie had a hobby." Though I thought I shouldn't be surprised. Everyone had a hobby.

"I'll let him tell you about it," Andrew said. "I think he's the only one who can explain it."

Apparently Charlie not only had a hobby, he had an unusual hobby. I would certainly be asking about that.

Andrew launched into story mode for a while. He told me again the one about him and his brother chasing rabbits and a few I hadn't heard. He stayed long enough to finish two cups of tea. I didn't finish my first one and planned to try a different flavor the next day. I had convinced Andrew to come back and help me work on the tea I bought so it didn't go to waste. He wouldn't commit to a standing tea time yet, but I planned to entice him with baked goods.

I would have all afternoon to learn how to cook. That wasn't a lot of time. I only needed to learn how to make one thing though. I wondered if it was weird that I was becoming friends with a man who was older than my dad who was older than most everyone else's dad. I didn't care if it was weird. I enjoyed his company.

My baking lesson was a bit tricky. I had no teacher and no ingredients. I spent a long time just reading through the recipes. Some used words like braise and dredge as though everyone knew what they meant and turned pipe into a verb. Some called for equipment I didn't know if I had. Some were just a list of ingredients with no instructions at all. Those famous cinnamon rolls appeared to take four hours to make, and that was for someone who knew what she was doing.

I found something promising called c.c. muffins. C. c. appeared to stand for chocolate chip. It was one that had no instructions, but the ingredient list was reasonably short. And I knew what a muffin pan looked like. I put the recipe in my pocket and drove to the store. I had only ever been to the store in the mornings and Mabel was surprised to see me.

"What's this, hon?" she asked. "You doing some baking?"

"I intend to try. I found a box of Aunt Rose's recipes."

"Good for you. A man can't resist a woman who knows her way around a kitchen."

She was talking about Charlie. My sudden interest in baking was going to feed the rumor. "I just thought the recipe sounded good," I said.

Mabel nodded knowingly. "You make him the cinnamon rolls next. Everyone loved Rose's cinnamon rolls. He'll be yours before the summer's over."

To get off the subject of Charlie, I decided to switch to a different rumor. "You know what? I thought I heard a scream coming from upstairs the other day."

Mabel put her hand over her mouth. "Oh, dear," she gasped.

"It turned out to be a bird outside the window. You and your talk of ghosts had me almost too afraid to go find the noise."

"Are you sure it was a bird?"

"I'm sure," I said. Mabel still looked skeptical. Skeptical enough to relay news of the scream to other ghost watchers around town. My work was done.

I went home to practice making muffins. It seemed simplest to add the ingredients in the order they were listed. I ended with something that I thought looked like muffin batter. Though I had never done any real cooking, I had occasionally wandered through the kitchen while my mom was cooking. Sometimes she asked me to stir things. I watched the muffins and the time closely to figure out how long to cook them.

I ate four muffins for dinner that night. I didn't want all of them to go to waste and, if I do say so myself, they were awesome. I put two in the fridge as an emergency backup and threw out the others. It was nearly bedtime when I realized that I hadn't checked my phone all day. When it showed two voicemails, I wondered if my parents wanted to know if they'd at least be invited to the wedding.

Neither message was a parent though. The first message was a woman named Sofia. She had been a pretty good friend during grad school. She got married a week after graduation and moved out of state with her new husband. I hadn't heard from her in a month and she was just checking in. I didn't feel like explaining my new living situation at the moment.

The second message was from Charlie. He said, "Hi, Rebecca. I was just wondering how that list is coming along. I wanted to encourage you to make it as long as possible. I wouldn't mind having more work than we can finish in a day. I'll call you on Friday as planned. Bye."

I had forgotten I was supposed to be making lists. At least I could add chocolate chip muffins to the one for Jill.

Chapter 11

I had started reading a few pages in my aunt's journal before bed each night. While I wasn't any more interested in the thought process behind which crops to plant, the style had me hooked. The garden seemed to be the most important thing in her life and yet the most common adjective she used for it was nice. The tomato plants had reached a *nice* height. The peppers were turning a *nice* shade of red. The corn had *nice* silk. It was completely devoid of passion and I knew if I kept a journal it would read the same way. Of course mine wouldn't even have a hobby.

Andrew had told me that only two things should provoke passion: God and people. I might understand what he meant on the first count. There had been moments in church when all five senses had been simultaneously touched – the taste of wine on my tongue, incense in the air, the kneeler beneath me, stained glass in front of me and beautiful music filling my ears. Those were moments when I thought I had a glimpse of passion. It felt like God's passion, something He merely let me share for that moment. It didn't feel as though it came from me.

People didn't inspire passion either, not in me. I mostly thought that people were nice to have around. I didn't find myself particularly attached to any of them. Each step of my life – high school, college, grad school – saw me swapping out one set of friends for another. And I never mourned the loss of the last set. I didn't even miss Jacob more than I missed anyone else.

Our relationship had been practically platonic. We shared only tight-lipped kisses and occasional hugs. Sometimes Jacob told me that he looked forward to things being different when we were married. But it never felt as though he was holding anything back. I liked that he felt safe. I also liked that he seemed just as staid as I was. I thought that made us a good match. When our relationship ended though, I got another glimpse of someone else's passion.

Charlie called me on Friday. The first thing he said was, "Hi. I have a bone to pick with you."

"Why?" I asked. I hoped he wasn't upset that I hadn't called him after Wednesday's message. He hadn't asked me to call back.

"Why is it that Grandpa gets to spend the week with you having tea parties and homemade goodies and I only get invited over for work?"

"Oh." I laughed slightly out of relief. "There are a few muffins left if you do a good job for me."

"At least I rate leftovers. Do you have a plan for what you want to do tomorrow?"

"I hoped maybe you'd be willing to help me sort through some boxes."

"Boxes?" he asked.

"Yeah, there's a ton of unlabeled boxes upstairs and I need to figure out if there's anything worth saving."

"Oh! A treasure hunt." Charlie sounded almost excited.

"Is a treasure hunt still fun if you don't find any treasure?"

"Sure."

"Hmm… sounds like your grandfather was right. He seemed to think you'd enjoy looking through boxes because of your hobby, but he wouldn't tell me what the hobby was."

"It's not really a hobby. Just something I like to do sometimes."

"And what is it that you like to do?"

"I, um, maybe I'll tell you about it later. What time should I come over tomorrow?"

I decided to let Charlie change the subject. It seemed that not only was his hobby unusual, it was somewhat embarrassing. I was very curious. I thought I'd have better luck getting it out of him in person. "I guess I'd be ready any time after 10:30 or so. Are there specific times you need to be with your grandfather?"

"Not really. 10:30 works well because my mom is supposed to pick him up just before then to take him to the city for an appointment with his doctor. She plans to take him to lunch afterward so they'll be gone about three hours or so."

"We have a plan then. See you in the morning, Charlie."

"Looking forward to it. Good night, Rebecca."

Charlie showed up at 10:15. I was still braiding my hair. I finished quickly and answered the door. I noticed his car in the driveway.

"You drove?" I asked as he came in.

"It's nearly 90 already."

"It's not much cooler in here, you know?"

"You don't have air conditioning?"

"Yeah, this house was built before air conditioning was invented."

Charlie chuckled at my condescension. He said, "I'm pretty sure this house was built before electricity and indoor plumbing, but it has those things."

"Good point," I conceded. "I guess no one thought AC was a necessity before now. You're not going to wilt and be useless after the first box, are you?"

"You do at least have a fan, right?"

I nodded. "I'll get it right now." The only portable fan was in my bedroom. Though I teased Charlie, I wished my house was cooler, too. I spent as much time as possible in the living room and the kitchen because those two rooms had ceiling fans. "Upstairs is this way," I said and motioned him to follow me through the living room. I thought we should get started.

I put the fan down to fiddle with the skeleton key. Charlie picked up the fan for me. "Why do you keep that locked?" he asked.

"It's a long story."

Charlie followed me up the stairs and into the bedroom with the mirror. He found an outlet for the fan and switched it on. I opened the closet door and said, "Ta-da!"

"Wow," Charlie gasped. "That's a lot of boxes."

"Still think it sounds like a treasure hunt?"

He smiled sheepishly. "I do. Aren't you interested?"

"I guess I am a little bit. I'm afraid it'll be nothing but decades-old clothing."

"Shall we find out?" he asked.

"Wait, we need one more thing." I ran down the stairs and found the box of markers I'd bought from Jill. When I returned, Charlie had taken down the first box. He was waiting for me to open it. I showed him the markers. "Even if we end up putting most of them back in the closet, I at least want them labeled."

He nodded. "This one wasn't too heavy. It might not be clothes."

I knelt beside the box and pulled off the lid. It was garland, red tinselly garland and green pine needle garland. At the bottom of the box were two strings of white lights. Christmas decorations weren't exactly treasure, nor were they trash. They wouldn't be useful for another six months. I labeled the box and pushed it aside. The next

55

two boxes were also Christmas decorations. One had ornaments for a tree and the other had miscellaneous items including stockings and a musical Christmas village I had seen spread out on the coffee table in years past.

Then we found a box of sweaters. They were clearly handmade by a beginner.

"Who's the knitter?" Charlie asked.

I could only shrug. "I'd have to guess Rose, but I don't remember anyone mentioning knitting."

"She may not have been ready to share. These don't look like the work of someone who's had much practice." He held up a rather oval-shaped brown sweater with one sleeve longer than the other. "I don't mean that to sound disparaging though," he added. "This is still better than I could do."

That reminded me of something. "Speaking of not wanting to talk about things, you were kind of evasive when I mentioned your hobby on the phone."

"Oh, you noticed that, huh?"

"Why don't you want to tell me?"

He sighed. "People just tend to laugh so try not to laugh too much."

"Okay." I put on a serious face. It made him laugh. "So you're allowed to laugh at me, but not the other way around?"

"Yes," he said. "That sounds fair."

I didn't say anything. I just waited for him to share.

"It's not a real hobby. Sometimes I just like to take things apart."

"What things?" I asked.

"Anything that might be interesting on the inside. Mostly electronics I guess. Some toys have cool mechanisms."

"Do you put them back together again?"

Charlie was running his teeth over the edge of his lower lip. It was cute that he cared about my reaction. "No. I pull out wires and dismantle anything I can. I'm not sure anyone could put things back together when I'm done with them."

"So you destroy things for fun?"

"I try to find things that are already broken."

"That is a little crazy. But I'm not going to laugh at you. I wish I had a hobby."

He tilted his head to consider me. "There's nothing that you like to do?"

56

"Nothing that's... I read a lot and I run every morning and sometimes I watch TV. Those are not hobbies though. I like running, but I do it to stay in shape. I read to find things out or pass the time. There's nothing that I do just because it's fun."

Charlie kept looking at me. Finally he said, "Fun doesn't have to happen all by itself. We're being productive right now and still having fun, right?"

Now it was my turn to reflect. Mostly because I was surprised to realize that I *was* having fun. Charlie kept getting this goofy expression on his face as though there was a chance we'd find the Holy Grail under the next ceramic Santa. I smiled at him. "Okay, you caught me having fun. Bring out the next box."

He nodded eagerly and turned to the closet while I drew a big X on the box of sweaters and started a trash stack.

"Man, this one weighs a ton." Charlie groaned as he slid the next box across the carpet rather than picking it up.

"Maybe this is a good one."

Charlie rubbed his hands together while I held the lid with both hands and paused to build suspense.

"Any time now," he prompted me.

"Okay... one... two... three!" I pulled off the lid.

"Blankets?" Charlie looked confused. Blankets should have been lighter. On top of the box was something pink and fuzzy. It had my name and date of birth embroidered on a corner.

"That's strange," I said. "This seems like something my parents would have."

"Your middle name is Anne?"

"That's what it says. What's yours?"

Charlie smiled at me and said, "Lately."

"If I didn't know that was a family name, I'd think it was funny."

Charlie was still smirking at me. "Why are you laughing if you don't think it's funny?"

"I'm sorry. It's just that you looked at me as though you expected me to laugh."

"What's under the blanket?"

I moved the blanket aside and found what appeared to be an album. It was too heavy to be pictures. I opened it up and found pages of coins. "This is actually kind of cool," I said. "I remember my dad talking about his dad's coin collection. This must be it."

57

"Do you think it's worth much?" Charlie's question was full of curiosity, not greed.

"I couldn't even guess. I doubt it's anything like a fortune though. My dad said that Grandpa had some semi-valuable coins, but that his collection was about variety over value. Like I know he tried to collect coins from as many countries as possible and that he saved coins as memories, too. My dad said that when he lost his first tooth, his dad traded him a dime for the nickel the tooth fairy had left."

Charlie laughed. "That's funny when you know who really gave him the nickel to begin with."

"Yeah, Dad said he tried to trade a few more nickels and his dad insisted only the first one was valuable enough to save." I turned only a few pages before I closed the album. I didn't really have time to study the contents at the moment. "I wonder if my dad would like to have these." As the thought came to me, I realized that I wanted to ask my dad about the coins. I didn't feel like snubbing him anymore. The anger towards my parents had vanished when I stopped thinking about it.

Charlie was watching me. I set the album aside. "So this is all coins?" I asked as I peeked into the box. There were several albums and nothing else. I put the lid back on and labeled the box. "If you could just push this over there for me I say we break for lunch next. What do you think?"

He said, "Is it cooler downstairs?"

Chapter 12

There had been a note on the back of the muffin recipe that suggested swapping the chocolate chips for raisins with cinnamon. I did that Friday morning and had a few left for me and Charlie. I also cut up two different fruits and put them in a bowl. It was almost a fruit salad and it was almost something you could offer to company. Charlie seemed to like it anyway. And he liked sitting under the ceiling fan.

The next box we opened did have clothes. I think they must have belonged to my grandfather. The box after that was more of his clothes. He had evidently been a larger man than my father. There would be another stop at the thrift store in my future. I didn't mind since what I hoped to find in the closet was space for those dining room chairs.

Charlie looked into the next box and asked, "What's this?" It seemed to be a lot of bunched up old newspapers. A bit of exploration revealed that the newspapers were protecting my grandmother's collection.

"It's salt and pepper shakers."

"How many salt and pepper shakers does a person need?"

"50."

"Why 50?" Charlie asked.

"This was my grandmother's thing. She was trying to collect a set from each state. My dad said he thought she had around 40. She stopped collecting them after my grandpa died."

"Do you think he'd want these, too? Or do you want them?"

"I don't know. And that's the worst thing we can find in any of these boxes. Things I don't know what to do with."

Charlie carefully rewrapped the cupcake-shaped shaker he was holding and set it in the box. "Should I put it with the coins for now?"

"Yeah, bring on the next one."

"This is another light one. What are the odds all forty salt and pepper shakers fit in that first box?"

"Do you want to open this one and find out?"

59

"They're your boxes."

"I insist you start taking turns. It's only fair since you're helping."

"All right." Charlie grabbed the lid and pulled it up slowly before he pushed it back down. He slowly started pulling it up again.

"Stop teasing me and open it."

He took the lid all the way off and we saw more newspaper. I checked to be sure and it was more shakers. Hopefully, the rest of them. I labeled it and Charlie brought me another box.

It was my turn to open this one. It was yarn… skeins and skeins of yarn in a rainbow of colors.

"I'm thinking someone gave up on the knitting," Charlie observed.

"You're probably right about that. I wonder if Jill could use these."

"Who's Jill?"

"Jill from 'Things to Do' in town. She's a knitter and maybe she could sell what she doesn't want."

"I don't think I've ever been in that store."

"I'm not surprised. I doubt she stocks anything broken for your hobby."

"Next box," Charlie said.

I made a new stack for Jill.

Charlie plopped a box in front of me. "Do I get another turn? I have a good feeling about this one." He had that look again of hopeful curiosity.

"Go ahead," I told him.

He pulled the lid off quickly and the curious expression stayed right where it was.

I began to sift through the items. The box contained about two dozen unopened and very old craft kits. The ones with copyright dates predated me. They were mostly needlepoint kits. There was one set of fabric picture frames, several circles for hanging, some loose lace and ruffles and almost everything in the box featured cats.

"Jill?" Charlie suggested.

I shrugged. "Why not? She probably won't want them, but she might get a kick out of them before I toss them."

Charlie moved the box. His phone rang before he could bring out another. "It's my mom," he said. "This'll just be a minute." I tried not to listen in on his side of the conversation. He mostly only agreed to things before he hung up anyway. "They're back at Grandpa's now. She said she'll stay with him until he feels like a nap and asked if I could plan on going back in about an hour so I'll be there when he wakes up. Is that okay with you?"

"Of course. I'm grateful for your help, but I know this isn't the real reason you're in town."

"I can't have two reasons?" His tone was teasing. His eyes sparkled with something else.

"Next box," I said.

He brought over another one.

"Whose turn is it?"

"Rock Paper Scissors?" Charlie suggested.

I nodded. "On three."

His paper covered my rock and he actually put his hand over mine for a moment. A frisson of that something else made me pull my hand away to tap on the box. He opened it and discovered more old man clothes. Then I opened a box just like it.

"More clothes?" Charlie asked as he opened the next one. He sounded a little disappointed for the first time. I looked in the box. On top of some neatly folded clothes was a mess of at least twenty neck ties. I picked up a fairly vile orange one with yellow stripes.

"You know, I haven't found anything for you yet. Maybe as a thank you for helping me you should go home with a few snazzy ties."

That made Charlie laugh. It was only fair as he'd been entertaining me for the last few hours. He said, "I'd rather have one of those scary sweaters."

I was still checking out the ties. "Actually, a few of these are not so bad. Do you ever wear ties?"

"Honestly? I usually wear one to church on Christmas and Easter and maybe the occasional wedding. I probably have more than I need already."

I found a plain dark green tie. "Christmas, huh? This green one would be appropriate." I held an end in each hand and flipped it over his head. I had thought his eyes were a light brown, but up close and next to the green tie they suddenly looked green. They were a very nice green. Something about those eyes made my heart beat faster. It was the fact that they were moving towards me. Charlie leaned over the box between us and tentatively touched his lips to mine. Then the kiss became less tentative and a tingly feeling spread from my lips through my whole body. It felt like an invisible hand pulling me closer to him.

61

I used my very visible hands to push lightly on his chest. He backed away and looked at me as though asking if he had done something wrong. I didn't know the answer. I said, "I just think we should get back to work for now."

He nodded and picked up the lid for the box of ties. I could see the smile he was trying to hide because his crease dimple kept popping out.

Under the next lid we found what I think Charlie had been hoping for all along. The box was crammed to the very top and contained the most random objects. There was an extension cord, a day planner from 1995, a mesh bag of marbles, a shoebox full of clothespins and a smiley face button pin. We found a pickle jar full of seashells, a can cozy with a bank logo on the side, and even a bicycle chain in a Ziploc bag.

"Why would anyone save any of this stuff?" Charlie asked. He was holding the jar of shells over his head so he could look at them through the bottom. He looked like someone trying to put together a fascinating jigsaw puzzle.

I pulled out a white apron and said, "Oh, look what I found." Beneath the apron, all wrapped in its own cord, was an old-style clock radio. It was the kind where the numbers flip down.

"Those are so cool on the inside," Charlie said.

"Do you want it?"

"It might not be broken." I could tell he wanted it.

I checked my watch. Charlie should be leaving soon. "No one needs this so you can have it if you promise to come back and help me again later."

"Okay." He took the clock. "How about if I keep Grandpa company through dinner and then come back for an hour or two this evening?"

When I said later, I had meant maybe the following Saturday. If he was eager to help though, then I was eager to continue our progress.

He came back about 6:30 and we found two more boxes of clothing, another box of miscellaneous items (of which I decided to keep only an unopened package of paper plates) and a box that held various holiday items, including a beautiful Easter tablecloth with matching cloth napkins. Before he left, Charlie said that Andrew had insisted on having me over for Sunday dinner. That was an offer I couldn't refuse.

Chapter 13

Sunday was a challenge for me. Most Sundays I only had to sit in the pew to feel like a good Christian. If I was lucky, there'd be a joke or two during the homily and the whole experience would be relatively painless. The Sunday I faced my parents required actual practicing. The way I figured it, there were four commandments on the line. Number four was the obvious one. I had not been honoring my parents by acting as though being sent to live off my significant inheritance while I figured out what to do with my life was some sort of child abuse.

Then there was the commandment about not bearing false witness. To avoid that I wouldn't be able to pretend my parents had been imagining my silent treatment. I'd have to work on the very first commandment in order to snub the god of pride. Pride didn't want me to admit I'd done anything wrong. And of course I couldn't very well keep the Lord's day holy if I was breaking all His rules.

I went in as the music began and squeezed into the pew next to my dad. He smiled and said nothing. My mom leaned around him and whispered, "Good morning, honey."

As we walked out I saw Charlie and Andrew with a few people who must have been other family members. Charlie waved and I waved back. My mom noticed this. In an unnecessarily dramatic stage whisper she said, "Rebecca, have you met someone? He's adorable!"

"Mom," I said, "he's a neighbor and he's only a friend." An unasked voice in my head reminded me that I didn't let my friends kiss me. I was working on a different honesty at the moment. My dad asked if I wanted to join them for lunch. They were happy to forget things had been weird, which I guessed they guessed was what I wanted. I wasn't going to let them let me off so easily.

"Guys, I'll join you for lunch, but first I have to say I'm sorry. I shouldn't have been, well, pouting for so long."

Mom nodded. "It's okay."

Dad said, "We knew you just needed some space. We are glad that you've decided to talk to us again though."

They were still letting me off easily, but it's not as though they could ground me or anything. We did go out to lunch and spent some time catching up.

Dad asked me if I'd found the key.

"What key?" I said.

"The key for the side door. I hung up the skeleton key so you could keep the inside one locked until we figured out who had the key. I know Hartford is pretty safe, but I'd feel better if we knew."

"Oh, yeah. I found it." I didn't tell him where I found it or that I was still keeping the inside door locked. I only wanted him to feel better. He also felt the same way I did about his parents' collections. He didn't really want to see them go, but he didn't want to be the one to have to store them either. I told him I'd keep them at least a while longer.

Charlie fired up the grill for dinner again. He made steaks that were very tasty and I had no idea you could do sweet potatoes on a grill. Andrew entertained us with more stories, and Charlie and I told him about some of the things we had found in the boxes. Charlie walked me home again. I told him how we had been spotted the previous week and we spent most of the walk trying to guess through which window someone might be watching while also trying not to be too obvious about looking at all the windows. I hoped he assumed the prying eyes were the reason I ducked inside my house so quickly when we got to the porch.

I made two trips to town on Monday, the usual run to the store and a second trip in my car in the afternoon. Jill was happy to see me enter, but also surprised.

"What are you doing here in the afternoon?" she asked. "And what is all this?"

I was carrying two boxes. I brought them to her checkout counter and set them on the floor nearby. Then I put just the one with yarn on the counter so it would be easier for her to look through. "Well," I said, "I've finally started to make some progress cleaning out my aunt's house and I found some things I thought you might be interested in." I took the lid off the yarn.

"Cool," she said and began moving the top layer to get a peek at the different colors and textures. "I could definitely work with this. How much do you want for it?"

"Nothing."

"Are you sure?"

64

"Yes. I just want it out of my house."

"Okay, thanks." Jill nodded towards the second box as she spoke. "Is this all yarn?"

I shook my head. "This one's a little different." I slid the yarn box over to show her the contents of my other box. "You probably won't even want these, but I couldn't resist showing you. What do you think of this?" I asked as I removed the lid.

Jill's mouth fell open in some sort of shock. I couldn't tell at first if it was agony or ecstasy. But then she broke out in a huge grin and said, "Vintage crafts! These are awesome!" She rummaged eagerly through the box before she turned to me. "I can have these?"

"Absolutely," I said.

"You know what I'm gonna do? I'm gonna put these around my store, unopened, as decorations. But I'd sell them if anyone asks."

"Great. There's a ton of stuff I need to get rid of and I wish I could find new homes for all of it."

"You should have a yard sale," Jill suggested.

"Oh, I should." I had so much stuff I didn't want and a lot of it wouldn't fit in my car. If I could get people to come and take it away… I should definitely do that.

"Okay," Jill said as she put down a puffy kitten pattern. "I'll leave these for later. We need to talk about you. How's your homework coming?"

"Not so good. I only have five things on the list." I'd actually thought of six. I didn't write down Charlie's dimple and she didn't need to know that.

"Five?" She looked at me incredulously. "Only five?"

I tried to shrug an apology.

She sighed heavily. "You're worse off than I thought. Cancel the homework. I think we're going to have to go trial and error." She held up her hand to indicate I should wait for her.

Her yellow and white polka dot socks were the last things I saw disappearing into another aisle. She returned with something behind her back. "Now you don't have to buy this if you don't want to, but this is what I recommend… that you *try* something."

She moved a very colorful box around to her front. "Origami," she said. "I know this says for kids, but that's just because it's beginner stuff. It has great instructions and the right paper all in the box. Sometimes one hobby can lead you to another because you'll realize that you want something more or less abstract or more visual or... do you get the idea?"

"I think so." I took the kit from her and looked it over. The monetary investment was minimal and it wouldn't make a mess or take up too much space in my house. Unless of course I made a lot of tiny paper flowers. "Okay, I'll try this." I brought it over to the counter. She waved me off.

"No charge. I consider all you brought me more than an adequate trade."

"Thank you. I'll let you know how this goes."

The rest of the week went very much like the previous one. And the week after that as well. My life was developing a happy rhythm. I tried a few more recipes for tea with Andrew. I also cheated and bought a few mixes. All the recipes and all the mixes made more food than two people could eat. Luckily, I found an outlet for the extras. Jill said that her husband worked with a bunch of guys who would eat anything. I brought the leftovers to her, which gave me an excuse to stop in her store even when I wasn't buying origami paper. I hadn't yet made it through what came in the box and was working up the courage to tell Jill that I probably never would.

Afternoons I spent working on the house. It was easier once Charlie helped me get started. I cleaned out that upstairs bathroom and tried to organize all the cupboards in the kitchen. Charlie and I found several photo albums and another of Rose's journals the next Saturday. The journal was from about 20 years ago. I read through it trying to find the passion in her life. If I could prove she felt something, then maybe there was hope for me.

Charlie was with me most of the day those two Saturdays. He helped me clean out more closets and figure out which furniture might go in my yard sale. I made sure we always had a table or something else solid between us. He didn't try to cross my barriers. I couldn't tell whether or not he knew I was intentionally placing them.

Sundays I had lunch with my parents. Our new relationship – the one where they cared about me instead of for me – was still solidifying. My mom was leaving me phone messages every day and I was trying to figure out how many of them to answer.

Sunday dinner was always fun. I met one of Charlie's two sisters the second week. She brought her husband and toddler with her. He was such a cute kid. I'd never been around babies so they kind of scared me. We sat on the floor playing with Andrew's dominoes for

66

half an hour and I didn't make him cry once. When Charlie tried to walk me home, his sister was leaving at the same time. I insisted he stay to say goodbye to her. The previous week it had been raining and he drove me. I got out of the car as soon as I could.

All in all, I was beginning to think my parents were on to something when they decided I should be a grownup. Then we had a holiday.

Chapter 14

July 4th is a big deal in Hartford. There's a parade in the morning, a street fair in the afternoon, a community picnic for dinner, and of course the day ends with fireworks. The parade was at 10 a.m. I wasn't particularly interested in watching it. Andrew wanted to go though and Charlie was coming to town a day early – the 4th was a Friday that year – and they both invited me to come along. It sounded as though I wouldn't be having a tea party so I thought I might as well watch a parade instead.

I had to make my run earlier than usual to be ready and the grocery store wouldn't be open. I ran in the other direction for a change. It felt weird. It felt as though I was going the wrong way.

Charlie and Andrew picked me up about 9:15 and we drove into town. We'd be early, but we wanted to get a good parking spot so Andrew wouldn't need to walk as far. Charlie carried a folding chair for Andrew. Charlie and I sat on the curb next to him. We talked about our plans for the rest of the day while we waited for the parade to begin.

"Count me in for the picnic," Andrew said. "You kids do the fair and the fireworks without me."

"I think I'd rather skip the fair, too," I said. "It's mostly junk food and kiddie games."

"Can I come over to work on the yard sale room then?" Charlie asked. We had removed everything from the emptiest room upstairs and were gradually filling it with items that could go in a yard sale. I had talked to Aiden when he came to mow the lawn and was prepared to pay him and as many friends as he could scrounge up to help us get it all outside when the time came.

"I guess so."

"You don't sound excited."

"You haven't noticed my lack of enthusiasm for moving furniture before now?"

"We could take the day off and do something fun. Maybe watch a movie?"

I looked at Charlie. He was very close to me on the curb and it was making me nervous. "No, you're right. We should keep going. Someday we might actually finish. If you came over right after lunch, how much time would we have before we'd need to get ready for the picnic?"

"Well..." Charlie narrowed his eyes at the ground. "We'd need to be there before five or we won't get a table. And I'll need time to shower and make the sandwiches..."

"What kind of sandwiches are we having?" Andrew asked.

"Roast beef, Grandpa, just like you requested. And Rebecca is bringing drinks and fruit salad."

Andrew nodded. "You should put a deck of cards in the picnic basket in case we have time to kill."

"Okay, I will." Charlie made a face that said he had heard that suggestion before. It was concern mixed with annoyance. Then he looked at me. "So if I left your place at 3:30 and came back for you at 4:30, would that give you enough time to be ready?"

"Sure. And while we're making plans, I think I'm getting brave enough to attempt the famous cinnamon rolls, but there's no way I could get them done before tea time. What would you guys think if I brought dessert on Sunday? Would it be weird to have cinnamon rolls for dinner?"

"Are you nuts?" Charlie asked. "There's never a bad time for cinnamon rolls."

"I might be a little later than usual though. I won't be able to start until after church."

"You know what, Charlie," Andrew said. "You should whip us up some bacon and eggs and do a whole breakfast thing for dinner."

"I could do that."

"And none of that turkey bacon." Andrew grimaced at me. "My doc wants me to give up real bacon, but I tell you what... God never meant for bacon to come from a bird."

I didn't know what to say to that. I *liked* turkey bacon. "But Charlie would have to give up the grill this week to make breakfast."

"What makes you say that?" Charlie asked.

"You can't cook eggs on a grill. Can you?"

He laughed. "You can make anything you want on a grill as long as you have enough tin foil."

The parade was pretty much what I expected; lots of old cars with flags, fire trucks with flags, and various local groups walking or riding

69

while waving flags. The high school marching band brought up the rear. They also had flags.

Charlie and I didn't get much accomplished in the afternoon. I made the mistake of untying a large rug so I could get a look at it before it went into the yard sale room. I still didn't want it after I saw the inside and it took us forever to get it rolled up as tightly as it had been.

Even though we were early, we got the last available table. There were seven picnic tables near some large trees on one side of the park. The trees provided some nice shade, but they would block the view for fireworks. Most people in town preferred to spread a blanket on the nearby hill for the picnic. They would leave the blankets to mark their places for the nighttime show. We hadn't specifically talked about it, but it seemed understood that Charlie and I would come back and watch the fireworks together. I was beginning to wonder if I could gracefully get out of it.

The picnic I enjoyed. I felt as though I was part of the town as the mingling began. Jack and Jill stopped by the table so he could thank me for the baked goods I'd been sending his way. Jill asked how the origami was coming.

I shook my head. "I suck. Last week I made a bird and asked Charlie if he could tell what it was. He thought it was an elephant."

"Remember you're a beginner." Jill squinted at me. "Enjoying the process is more important than the end product."

"Lately I've been finishing each project by crumpling it into the smallest ball possible and it still doesn't relieve my frustration."

"Okay," she said. "Maybe it's time to try something else. Come by the store soon. I'm thinking calligraphy or perler beads."

I didn't know what perler beads were. I considered calligraphy. I imagined myself starting a journal like my aunt's and filling it with very fancy words that still described a life full of nice.

An older couple stopped to say hi to Andrew and then a guy recognized Charlie from high school and sat down at our table. He recognized me as "that girl who runs through town in the mornings" and said he was glad to put a name with my face.

"Hilson?" he said. "Isn't that the name of the woman who lived in the haunted house?"

"Rose Hilson was my aunt. Her house isn't haunted though. I'm living there now."

"I don't know," our visitor said, "we used to go out there all the time. Did you ever see a ghost over there, Charlie?"

Charlie shook his head.

"I guess you were in a different crowd." The guy seemed to dismiss Charlie at that point and focus on me. "That was the thing to do on Halloween. Pretty much all of October actually. We'd drive slowly past the house and the braver kids snuck up to the backyard from the creek back there. Everyone had stories of the spooky things they'd seen."

"Like what?" I asked.

"Are you sure you want to know? With you living there and all?"

I nodded. I really wasn't sure I wanted to hear spooky things about my house. But I was curious and it wouldn't be the first time.

"Mostly just things moving in the windows and stuff we convinced ourselves was the old woman who lived there. One guy though swears he saw a light come on upstairs while she was sitting on the front porch."

I was about to say that didn't sound like anything too scary when Mabel came up to our table. "Tell him about your encounter with the ghost," she said.

"You saw something?" he asked.

Charlie was looking at me with surprise, too. He probably wondered why I hadn't told him this story.

"I didn't see anything," I said.

Before I could finish, Mabel said, "And neither could the cops. It had to have been the ghost."

"You had cops at your house?" Charlie asked.

I held up my hands to try to get everyone to let me talk. "It was no big deal. I was alone and thought I heard footsteps. I let my imagination convince me that someone had broken in. There was no one there. Alive or not." I was sure that was one time when concealing the truth was the right thing to do. I didn't want anyone, least of all Andrew, to know who had scared me.

Mabel said, "I understand why that's what you want to believe," before she waved at us and moved on to greet those at the next table.

The extra guy stood then as well. "Glad to have met you, Rebecca Hilson. If you do ever get scared or just lonely in that house by yourself, you can give me a call." He fished a business card out of his pocket and placed it on the table next to me. "Later, Charlie," he said as he left.

Charlie gave a slight scowl at the guy's back. The older couple had moved on while we were talking and Andrew began to chuckle softly. "Rose sure loved to scare those kids," he said.

"What do you mean?" I asked him.

"She looked forward to it every year. I don't know how people got started talking about that house being haunted. Once Rose got wind that kids were looking to be scared though, I tell you what… she was happy to oblige."

"What did she do?"

"All kinds of stuff. She had an oscillating fan behind the bedroom curtains and a light on a timer so it would turn on and off while she was outside. She used to drag a tape player on an extension cord way out in the back yard. The tape was mostly silence with occasional thumps and moans." Andrew smiled as he remembered. "One year she even tied a sack of flour in a tree. Strung it all the way to the house and she sat watching out the window for kids to assemble at the edge of the lawn. Then she untied the string. The flour hit the ground with a thud and sent a cloud of whiteness into the moonlight. Those kids skedaddled. And Rose laughed, laughed herself to tears when she told me about it."

"Wow," I said. "And nobody knew she was just playing tricks?"

"I bet some of the kids knew. But you know when kids are looking to be scared they see what they want to see."

Charlie was shaking his head. "That's so funny. I bet Mom didn't know. I almost went to the house once and Mom found out and insisted I not bother 'that nice lady.' Now I find out she would have been waiting for me."

"Rose never minded the mischief," Andrew said. "Even the few times her house was rolled, she figured she deserved it for giving the young'uns a fright."

A few other people waved as we left to take Andrew home. We stopped at my house and Charlie asked what time I wanted him to come back.

"Aren't you getting a bit tired of driving back and forth?" I asked

"No. Do you want to watch the fireworks?"

"I guess."

"If you want to go, then I want to take you."

I agreed and said goodnight to Andrew. Charlie came back an hour later and we drove to town for the third time. When we parked, he nodded to a blanket in the back seat. "Do you think there's any chance we'll find a place to sit?"

"I doubt it. The grass was pretty thoroughly covered when we left." This was true and I was glad it was true. The thought of sitting on a blanket with Charlie was... well, even in the midst of a crowd it would be way too close to romantic.

"You're probably right," he said. "I guess we'll just have to stand."

There was a paved path behind the hill. Late-comers and people who didn't want to sit on blankets for whatever reason were lining up along the path. As I took a place next to Charlie, I remembered standing along that same path for fireworks several years earlier. My parents and my Aunt Rose were sitting in folding chairs and I was standing behind them. They had offered to bring a chair for me. I was in high school though and thought if I was standing people might not assume I was there with the three old people. It didn't work. They kept turning around to talk to me. Specifically, I remembered Rose turning to me after an especially loud and deep explosion. She had said, "I like the ones you can feel."

I had agreed with her. I liked the chest-shaking booms. Now I wondered if I needed to have my heart shaken now and then to remind myself that I had one. It didn't seem to feel anything else. That was why I was afraid to start something with Charlie. There was no doubt I was attracted to him. I thought about trying to get him to kiss me again more often than was healthy. But it wasn't fair to risk his heart if mine couldn't break.

He nudged my arm with his and asked, "You all right?"

I realized I was staring at a tree in the distance. "Yeah, I was just thinking... remembering a time I was here before."

"Did you come to the Hartford display a lot when you were in the city?"

"A few times. I'm not sure when I was last here."

"I wonder if we've ever been here at the same time before."

I thought about that. I was trying to remember specific years I had been there when a voice called out, "Hey, you two! I'm keeping an eye on you so I can report back to Andrew if there's any funny business." It was Mabel. She was sitting with several other people on a blanket not too far in front of us. The people with her snickered at her comment.

I simply said, "Hi, Mabel."

Charlie looked a bit embarrassed. The sky crackled just then and was quickly followed by the first flash of the night. There were some pops and then a burst of light that seemed to fill the sky and I knew the boom was coming and it startled me anyway. Charlie gave me enough of a smirk to dent his cheek and then gave my hand a squeeze. He didn't let go. I began to panic. I wanted him to hold on and I knew I shouldn't want that. I pretended I needed that hand to scratch my leg. Then I folded my arms against the non-existent chill. Charlie stayed very focused on the display after that.

He was quiet when he drove me home, too. It felt as though we had argued. I tried to ignore the tension and asked him if he liked the fireworks.

He shrugged.

"I like the big booms even though they always startle me."

He stayed quiet. He looked like someone who had something to say. He said nothing.

I kept trying. "What, um, what time should I expect you tomorrow?"

He shrugged again and said, "The usual I guess."

I thanked him for taking me before I got out of the car. I was on my porch before I realized that he had also gotten out of the car and was jogging up behind me.

"Rebecca, wait... please wait."

I turned to face him. He seemed to be working up the courage to say what he wanted to say. Finally, he started talking in a rush. "Look, you're probably not doing it on purpose, but you're confusing the heck out of me. You always seem happy to have me around, but only as long as you can keep me at arm's length. You've got to know that I... is this where I get the just friends speech?"

I shook my head instinctively because his eyes were pleading against a just friends speech.

"Is there anything I should know?"

"What do you mean?"

"I don't know. Just anything that doesn't have to do with me, like an old boyfriend still in the picture or something."

"No, there's nothing like that."

"Then why... why does it feel like you keep trying to get close and then backing off? Was the first kiss that bad?"

I shook my head again and looked at the floor of the porch, partly because I didn't know what to say and partly because I knew I blushed

74

whenever I thought about that kiss. "I'm just not sure… I don't want you to get hurt."

Charlie put his hand up and ran his fingers through my hair. "I meant to tell you that your hair looks pretty this way." I had left it down for a change. He kept his hand near the ends and gently twisted the locks between his fingers. I inhaled deeply and forced my eyes up. I couldn't make them go any higher than the collar of his shirt when he was so close.

"Rebecca?" he said.

I refused to make eye contact. I was afraid that if I met his gaze he would kiss me. And I wouldn't have the guts to stop him.

"You do at least sort of like having me around, don't you?"

That was an easy question even when he was too close for me to think straight. "Of course I like having you around."

"And you're not completely put off by the idea that we might… possibly… someday… be more than friends?"

"No."

"Okay, how about this?" Charlie removed his hand from my hair and all the shivers left with it. He took a small step backwards. "If I promise to hang back here in friend zone for a while, will you promise to let me know when or if I no longer have to?"

"I… I can agree to that."

"I'll see you tomorrow then."

He waved as he walked back to his car. I breathed a sigh of relief. It was good to have things settled between us even if it was only a temporary settlement.

Chapter 15

Charlie kept his word the next day. We finished with the furniture in the stuffed bedroom and began to pull boxes out of that closet. Some of those boxes were labeled, but we went through them anyway to make sure the contents hadn't changed. I never once felt as though I needed to guard against an advance. A less frigid person would have been disappointed.

I sat with my parents at church again. Afterwards, my mom asked if I was eating well by myself. My dad wanted to know if I'd had any trouble with the ancient washing machine. The relationship had shifted a little, but they were still my parents. We did a fast food lunch so I could get home and start working on the cinnamon rolls.

In the times when the yeast was doing its thing, I checked on the progress upstairs. Charlie and I had dismantled the twin beds in the far bedroom before we converted it to the yard sale room. The pieces and the mattresses were now taking up more floor space in the guest bedroom than the mirror had. I couldn't decide whether or not I wanted to keep those beds. Bedrooms usually had beds in them, but maybe I didn't want to call that a bedroom. Maybe it could be my hobby room. I could display all my paper creations, labeled with blotchy calligraphy so people could tell what they were. I hadn't even tried calligraphy yet and I was imagining I'd be bad at it.

I stared at those beds and asked myself if I needed a pair of twin beds. That answer was obvious. One person did not need more than one bed. I was already keeping the guest bedroom set up in case my parents needed a place to stay. Even that was a stretch given how close their house was to mine. I asked myself if I wanted the beds and felt a twinge of something new, a desire to not always be a family of one. I didn't know if I should want that or not, but I made the decision to keep the beds anyway. My origami didn't need its own room. It only needed its own trash can.

The cinnamon rolls were just as good with tea the next day. I popped them in the microwave for a few seconds to fake a fresh-from-

76

the-oven warmth. The tea wasn't any better with cinnamon rolls than anything else. I just couldn't seem to develop a taste for it.

The day after that Andrew let himself in through the side door. I had stopped expecting him to do that. I was still in the habit of unlocking the inside door though. He walked right into the living room and asked where my parents were.

"My parents?" I asked.

"Yes," he said. "I shouldn't be here if they're not home, Rose. People will talk."

He meant Rose's parents. "They'll be here soon," I said. I hoped maybe the heat on the walk had affected him and that he'd figure out I wasn't Rose if he relaxed under the ceiling fan.

"Are you sure?" he asked.

"Please sit down. I'll get you some water."

I brought back a glass and he startled when I tried to hand it to him. I placed it on the table in front of him. He was quiet for what felt like a long time. He was so full of stories that the quiet was more unnerving than his apparent confusion. I suggested he have some of the water and he sipped from the glass fairly automatically. He seemed to come around as we sat together. He started talking anyway.

"We didn't think anyone would understand. People do talk, you know. But we wanted... eventually. We had our own lives. It seemed like the best way to add each other without trying to make one life."

"Andrew, do you want me to call Charlie?" I asked. I didn't know if that would do any good, but I felt rather in over my head.

"Charlie's a good boy. He already does too much for me. You shouldn't bother him."

I thought it was a good sign that he knew who Charlie was.

"Did he tell you how he stayed with me when he was in high school?"

And he also knew that Charlie was no longer in high school.

"There was a girl, you know," Andrew continued. "I don't remember her name. But that girl was the main reason he wanted to stay in Hartford. He waited the whole year, trying to get up the nerve to ask her out. Then someone else beat him to it. He never told his parents, but he told me." Andrew's face showed pride at the bond. He told me a little more about that year Charlie stayed with him. He had spent a lot of time teaching Charlie how to use the grill. And that there had been a time Charlie thought curfew didn't apply to him. Andrew insisted that was a mistake he made once.

I had made strawberry scones and I served them with water because it just didn't feel like a day for a hot beverage. Andrew didn't mention tea. He left abruptly, as though he suddenly became uncomfortable. I watched through the window to make sure he turned the right way to go home.

I hoped Andrew just had an off day. He came to the side door again the following day. In between thoughts that made sense, he kept saying that he wanted to see Rose. That was worse than when he thought I was Rose. The day after that he didn't show up at all. I wasn't sure what to do, but it seemed as though I should check on him. Maybe he was sick. Maybe he had been coming down with something and that had been what caused his confusion.

Before I knocked on his red door, I peeked in the window on the right side of the porch. He was sitting in that room watching TV. He looked comfortable and was sipping a diet soda. I decided not to bother him. If he had simply forgotten our appointment, I didn't want to upset him.

I called Charlie a bit later, trying to hit his lunch hour.

"Hi, Rebecca," he answered. "What's going on?"

"Hey, Charlie. I'm sorry to bother you…"

He cut me off. "It's not a bother. I like hearing from you."

"I just… I thought you should know that I'm worried about your grandfather."

"Oh. Has he been weird with you, too?"

"Yeah, he seems more forgetful and less… coherent."

"My mom and my aunt are worried, too. They've both called me saying how they hated to leave him in the mornings. They didn't really expect me to be able to do anything about it. I think they wanted to prepare me for what might be a rough weekend."

"You should probably plan on staying with him all day Saturday."

"Maybe I'll just sneak out while he's napping and find out what's in your box of miscellaneous supplies. You haven't looked without me, have you?"

"No, I'm still waiting for you."

"Excellent. I'll call you tomorrow when I get in."

Charlie hung up and went back to work. At least I assume he did work while at work. I knew Andrew needed him more, but I'd gotten used to spending my Saturdays with Charlie and it was regrettable that I might not see as much of him. I assumed I was still invited for Sunday dinner and would have to settle for that.

Charlie had found the box labeled "misc. supplies" in one of the bedroom closets. We had each other near hysterics guessing increasingly bizarre types of supplies that might be in the box. Eventually we decided that we didn't want to know yet. We decided that would be the last box we opened. When we had no other boxes to open or furniture to move, then we'd find out about the miscellaneous supplies.

Andrew came to tea on Friday and seemed pretty much his regular self. He called me Rose a few times, but I think that was because I looked like Rose and not because he thought I was my aunt. He apparently went to bed fairly early that night because Charlie called and asked if he could come see me for a bit in case he couldn't get away on Saturday.

Heavy rainclouds had arrived shortly before Charlie so when I opened the door for him I had a slight flashback to the night we met. "I felt a couple of drops," he said as he came in. "I think I just beat the storm."

"Maybe you shouldn't have come. I'd hate for you to have to go back in a downpour."

"Maybe I'll just be stuck here until it stops." He smiled a friendly, joking smile at me. I realized how much I had missed that smile and those happy green eyes while I'd been stressed about Andrew during the week. I suddenly wanted Charlie to kiss me. I wanted him to grab me like in the movies and kiss me before I could change my mind. He walked past me to the living room like a good friend.

A minute later I was glad he did that. I knew we couldn't unring that bell more than once. We talked for a while about Andrew and about a few things Charlie had to put up with at work. I told him how Mabel told me one of my neighbors had insisted she'd seen a little girl running through my backyard and that the child had vanished before her eyes.

Charlie laughed. It was good that he wasn't into ghost stories either. I didn't like to be scared. Then Charlie said, "If I could come over for only one thing tomorrow... I think I'll probably only have a half hour or so and if there was only one thing I'd have time to help you with, what would it be?"

And because I had just thought about being scared I said, "The attic."

"The attic?" he repeated. "You said we didn't need to worry about that before. What sort of work needs to be done? If it's full of stuff, I'm thinking that will be more than a half hour."

I shrugged at him. "I don't know. I've been too chicken to even look up there because I'm worried there might be spiders or other yucky stuff. But I think I should at least peek up there before the yard sale in case there's something I might be able to sell."

"Okay, so tomorrow I'll come over only long enough to protect you from spiders and yucky stuff. But you better have a good weapon handy for the spiders. I don't like them either."

The next day I almost brought my monster shovel in from the garage as a joke. Instead I handed Charlie a flyswatter before he led the way up the stairs. There was one small, round window in the attic that let in barely enough light that we didn't need flashlights. Of all the things I imagined we might find in the attic, what we actually found was the most surprising. Nothing. Unless you count the blistering heat, there was nothing at all in the attic. It was a small room with particle board floors and a sloped ceiling that met each side wall at about three feet high. The attic made the rest of the house feel breezy and pleasant. Charlie and I stood on the steps that came out in the middle of the room and looked around in disbelief. The house had closets and closets of boxes and a completely empty attic. That was weird. But at least it was one less thing for me to be afraid of.

Chapter 16

"One of the Casey boys is in a cast," Mabel told me as she scanned a container of blueberries. "He and his brother were wrestling around on the top bunk and he fell and broke his arm."

"That's too bad," I replied. I didn't have to know the Casey family to agree that a broken arm was bad news.

"And Mary Katherine told me that her youngest is going all the way to Texas for school this fall."

I simply nodded as I slid my card through the card reader.

"Oh, I never asked how you and Charlie liked the fireworks."

"They were great. How did you like the show?"

"Even better than last year's," she said. Mabel had been talking up the previous year's fireworks in the days leading up to the 4th. I waved as she turned her attention to someone behind me.

I had put off seeing Jill for a week and she was ready for me. The cacophony of her door had barely died down when she was standing in front of me with a book in one hand and a small box in the other. "This is the pen you want," she said. "It has black ink which is the most elegant. And I think you'll like this book. It has thick pages so the ink won't bleed through when you trace the letters. It has three different letter styles and lots of space for practice."

I wasn't going to put up a fight. Jill sensed my hesitation though.

"I don't mean to pressure you," she said. "I think this might work for you, but if you already know you won't like it, we can keep looking."

I shook my head. "No, I want to try this. These letters look cool." I was flipping through the book she had handed to me. "My concern though is that it won't work as a long-term hobby."

"Why not?"

"What do I do after I've figured out how to make all the letters?"

Jill didn't say anything. She scrunched up her forehead as though she didn't even understand the question.

I tried again. "I mean, once I can make the letters well and without looking at the book, what do I actually write with the fancy letters?"

"Everything!" Jill said.

"Everything?"

"Of course. Everything looks better with a little calligraphy. Letters to friends, recipes, scrapbooks are awesome... and Christmas cards! You send cards with 'Merry Christmas' in calligraphy and people know you mean it."

"All right. I'll start with those letters so I'll be able to send you a card."

Jill scanned the items for my new hobby and I traded them for a box of muffins. She also gave me an empty container to refill. When I got home, I put honey biscuits in the oven and tried to take my shower extra fast. The biscuit bottoms were just a little too dark. I put those aside for the guys I'd been told would eat anything. The second pan I watched closely while I prepared the tea tray. Andrew knocked on the front door. He was staring absently at the side of my porch when I opened the door.

"Andrew?" I said, trying not to sound as though I was concerned.

"Oh, hello, dear. You may need to get James out here to power wash your porch for you."

That was good. He wasn't lost in a different era, he was merely distracted by the filth on my house. "Come on in," I said.

He took his usual chair while I turned on the tea kettle.

"How are you today, Andrew?"

"My boy Charlie takes good care of me. I give him a hard time about being a babysitter, but I do enjoy his company. The house was very quiet this morning."

"I'm sorry I've been taking him away to help me over here."

Andrew looked at me for a few seconds, seemed to be studying my face, before he said, "So when are you two getting hitched anyway?"

"Hitched?" I repeated. I wasn't sure if he was teasing or if perhaps he had forgotten that Charlie and I had known each other only a little more than a month. And we weren't even dating anyway.

"You can't wait around too long," Andrew said. "I want to be there."

"Andrew, I'm going to be completely honest with you."

"Good," he said. "It's better than beating around the bush any day."

"The truth is that Charlie and I are friends. We are not talking about getting married. But if we ever decide to get hitched, you will have a place of honor at the ceremony."

82

I left him smiling as I answered the call of the whistling kettle. Once he had his tea bag brewing he said, "Did I ever tell you about the time William jumped off the roof?"

I'd have let him talk even if he had, but I was pretty sure I was about to hear a new story.

"William was mostly a pretty smart kid. But there were times when you would have guessed he wasn't all that bright. This one time he'd been looking at pictures of paratroopers and he figured that if guys could jump out of airplanes then all he'd need to make it off the roof of the shed was a bed sheet. I tried to tell him it wouldn't work and he wouldn't listen. And you know what? Even though I knew it wouldn't work I still stood there and watched. William climbed up on the roof with his sheet. He tied the corners under his armpits and he jumped." Andrew paused for a few sips of tea and for dramatic effect. "He dropped like a stone. One side of the sheet came untied and he landed on a glass bottle. Now he was barefoot and that bottle broke and went right up through his foot."

I winced. This sounded worse than falling off a bunk bed.

"So William gets up and he's standing there in the yard. He has a bed sheet still hanging off one shoulder and there's a piece of glass about three inches long sticking out of his foot and you know what he says to me?"

I shook my head.

Andrew took another sip of tea. "He says to me, 'Don't tell Mom.' Now he was afraid that if Mom saw his foot she was gonna get out the turpentine. You know I had to tell our mama anyway. She was pretty sharp. She was gonna notice if one of her sons was limping around on a bloody foot. I figured it was best if we owned up to it before she found out on her own. Of course she did douse him with the turpentine. Before and after she yanked the glass out of his foot. William howled and I didn't blame him. Mama said it served him right for actin' like he didn't have a lick of sense."

Andrew knew how to tell a story. Some people might have said, "My brother once cut his foot jumping off a roof." That was a fact, not a story. He told a few more before he had to leave.

I noticed that he had taken to calling me dear all the time instead of asking my name. I hoped that was at least in part because I was starting to feel as much like family to him as he was to me. I had never known either of my grandfathers. Andrew was giving me a taste of what I didn't know I was missing.

83

He was late for tea on Tuesday. I was starting to worry. Charlie had said on Sunday that he wasn't sure it was necessary for him to have stayed all day Saturday after all. And Andrew had seemed fine since then. We thought his bad days were over. It was going to bother me all day if I didn't check on him though.

I was walking between our houses when I got a frantic call from Charlie. "Rebecca," he said, "are you busy right now?"

"Not exactly. I was…"

He cut me off before I could explain where I was headed. "Grandpa got lost."

"Lost?" I repeated. I stopped walking and just listened.

"I guess he went for a walk this morning and he ended up at the house where he grew up. The people who live there now didn't know what else to do so they called the police. Grandpa couldn't tell them where he lived so they took him to the station and they want a family member to pick him up. My aunt is coming, but she's on the other side of the city so it'll take her forty minutes to get over there. I wanted to ask you if you could go sit with him until she gets there. Please can you do that?"

"Of course I can. I was worried anyway. I'll go right now." I jogged back to my house and took my car to the police station. I found Andrew right away. He looked like a small, frightened child in an old man's body. There was an officer sitting next to him.

The officer looked at me, "Are you his family?"

"No, but they asked me if I could sit with him until someone can get here. Is that okay?"

"You can have my seat. I'll be right over there if you need anything." He stood and pointed to my left before walking that way.

I took the vacated seat next to Andrew. I wasn't sure what to say to him.

"I want to go home," Andrew said.

"I know, and you will. We're just going to wait here for a little while first."

"I want to go home," he repeated.

"You will, Andrew."

He looked at me for the first time when I said his name. His eyes had that same look as the first time I met him, confusion and fear. "Rose?" he asked. "Why can't I go home?"

"Soon, Andrew, soon. Do you remember… do you remember when those girls took your clothes when you were in the pond with William?"

Andrew smiled vaguely. "That was William's idea."

"The water felt cool on a hot day," I said. "Even if you were afraid of getting in trouble."

"Yeah, you were there, Rose. You were an angel that day. You were an angel the day you pushed me into the pond, too."

"I don't remember that story."

"How could you forget, Rose? That was the first time I proposed."

"It was a long time ago."

"You're still an angel," he said. The fear was gone from his eyes, but the confusion lingered. He sat there staring at the floor and he was so calm I decided to sit quietly myself. I watched feet walking past us in between glimpses at the large clock on the wall. Eventually a pair of feet stopped in front of us. It was the cop who looked like a teenager. I think Mabel had said his name was Jimmy. He was holding two paper cups of water and he offered one to Andrew and one to me.

"Thanks," I said.

"You and Charlie must be getting serious if he has you looking after his grandfather."

"Andrew and I are friends," I said by way of explaining without really explaining. There was nothing like trying to figure out how you felt about a guy while surrounded by people who were also trying to figure out how you felt about him.

The young officer nodded at Andrew. "I hope he's going to be okay."

"He's fine," I said defensively.

"Well, let me know if you need anything." He walked away and I felt bad about snapping. I went back to examining the pattern on the floor.

Andrew sighed next to me before he said, "They're going to put me away after this."

"Maybe not," I said.

"I won't put up a fuss. Maybe it's time."

There wasn't anything I could say to that. All I could think was that I was glad I wouldn't be involved in a decision. Acceptance was easier than responsibility. I thought about the fact that my own parents were not much younger. Fortunately, Charlie's aunt showed up to distract me from those thoughts.

She waved to us and then stopped to speak with someone at a desk for a moment. When she came closer, she knelt in front of Andrew and said, "Dad, are you ready to go home?"

He nodded. He didn't say anything.

She looked at me next. "You must be Rebecca."

"Yes. Rebecca Hilson."

"I'm Margaret. Thank you for coming. How's he doing?"

"Just a little quiet."

I walked out to the parking lot and said goodbye. I thought my tea parties might be over.

Chapter 17

I sat at my kitchen table after dinner and opened the calligraphy book for the first time. I flipped through it back and forth and examined the different letters, trying to figure out which style might be the easiest. Then I closed the book and decided to start at the beginning. The first few pages were lessons on holding the pen and different strokes. I didn't have a lot of patience with those pages. I managed to make a few As that looked like As before I moved on to Bs. C was easy. Once I could do that one I skipped ahead to see how to make an H. Then I made an A and an R.

I put down the pen at that point and washed my inky fingers before I pulled out my phone. I thought about telling him the truth... that I just wanted to hear his voice. I knew that would sound corny. I asked if his grandfather's incident had prompted another family meeting.

"Not exactly," he said. "I think we've turned into a dictatorship. My aunt called my mom and said she was tired of worrying and trying to get to town before work in the morning and they had to get Grandpa somewhere safe."

"So that was the decision?"

"Pretty much. But I think it might be best. My mom called me after she had talked to both of her sisters and it sounded like she'd been looking into places already. I think it's been on everyone's mind."

"Have they picked a place then?"

"Yeah, it's called Riverwoods. He moves in about two weeks from now. Aunt Margaret is staying with him the rest of this week and Mom took next week off work for her turn."

"Does that mean... are you still coming for the weekend?"

"Sort of. My aunt offered to stay through the weekend and I asked if she could just take Saturday so maybe we could do something."

"What do you have in mind?"

"I'm sorry. I did mean something specific. I didn't mean to sound like I was asking you out. That's not a friend thing. I... Well, I want to check out this Riverwoods place and I hoped maybe I could talk you into going with me. I know it's kind of a big favor."

"Are you kidding? After all the stuff you carried and sorted for me? I owe you several big favors by now. And I'd like to see the place anyway. I'll need to know where it is so I can visit."

"Great." Charlie sounded relieved. "Can I pick you up about 1 o'clock on Saturday?"

"I'll be ready."

"What are you doing tonight?" he asked.

"Well, I saw Jill this morning so I'm trying a new passion."

"Calligraphy?"

"Yes."

"Anything sparked yet?"

"So far all I can say is that I like it better than origami."

"No elephants?"

"It wasn't an elephant."

"What are you writing?"

"I'm just practicing the letters first."

"Then what?"

"I asked Jill the same thing and she said that everything is better with calligraphy."

"Well, of course." Charlie's sarcasm came through the phone clearly. "Just think how much nicer all those boxes upstairs would look if you had known calligraphy last month."

"That's funny, Charlie. You're going to be sorry you mocked this when I start to love it."

"I don't think I have anything to worry about."

Of course he didn't. I didn't love anything. "What about you? Have you taken anything apart lately?"

"No, actually. Not since that clock radio you gave me."

"What have you been doing with yourself then?"

"You mean besides spending my weekends in Hartford?"

"Right. I guess Andrew and I have been keeping you pretty busy."

"Would I be breaking our agreement if I said you were far more interesting than the inside of an old TV?"

"No. Because there is nothing remotely romantic about being compared to the inside of an old TV."

"Good. Because you are. I'm glad you called."

"Me, too. I'll see you Saturday."

Charlie hung up and then called me back a few minutes later. He wanted to tell me that I probably wouldn't see Andrew the next day. Charlie had told his aunt about our standing tea time and she said that she didn't want to bother me. I supposed I was going to have to give up the visits soon anyway. I would still be able to see Andrew and I might even be able to do it without pretending to like tea. But I was concerned about the broader implications. The nice pattern I had been trying to call a life was about to change.

I wondered most of all what the change would mean for me and Charlie. It felt as though I suddenly had a deadline for figuring out how he fit into my life. He was only going to spend two more weekends down the street from me. I wasn't sure I could ask him to drive from the city only for me if I couldn't offer him some sort of clarity. And if I told him we'd only ever be friends… I didn't think he'd be okay with that.

I had been looking for clarity and direction since I moved into Rose's house. The quest was suddenly more urgent. I needed to know if my relationship with Charlie could or should go beyond friendship. That would eventually lead to marriage. I still didn't know if I wanted to get married at all. I closed my eyes and asked God if marriage, a lifetime union of one person's hopes and dreams to another, could possibly be right for me… a person who didn't have any hopes or dreams. He was silent on the subject as usual so I turned to the next best authority on major life decisions: the Internet.

I thought I might be able to find a survey or quiz, something with simple answers that would decide for me if I was meant to be alone. The search results I found, however, were mostly aimed at couples. There were plenty of surveys and quizzes for compatibility for people who had already decided in favor of marriage and just needed to know if they had picked the right person.

But as I looked over the questions, I realized that they were still things that I needed to ask myself. I spent a lot of time with those questions – and reviewed my answers with God – over the next few days. I ended up with two conclusions. The first was that I did want to get married and have a family. The second was that I couldn't have what I wanted. I was too much like my aunt. I liked Charlie and he did something to me, something that made my skin tingle. But those were nice feelings, not passionate feelings. Charlie deserved love.

By the time Saturday rolled around, I had filled my entire calligraphy book with practice letters and moved on to writing random notes to myself on the leftover origami paper. I wrote my mini shopping lists in curly letters instead of keeping them in my head. "Broccoli" actually looked very cool in calligraphy. "Laundry soap" still looked ordinary.

I had finished lunch and had nothing else to do before Charlie picked me up. I grabbed the pen from the counter and some paper and tried to think of what to write. It must have been because I was going to see him soon that Charlie was the only thing I could think about. I found myself writing "I love you, Charlie," just to see what that would feel like. It felt foreign. I did not come from a demonstrative family. Except for that day my mother sobbed about all her failings, we didn't normally do things like go around expressing our feelings. I crumpled up the note, which wasn't true anyway, and dumped it in the trash. Then I sat down and wrote my own name over and over.

I filled two pieces of paper before Charlie knocked. He was wearing a shirt with a collar like he did on Sundays and it made me feel less self-conscious about my decision to wear a dress. I really didn't know what one wore to visit a nursing home.

"Wow. You look nice," Charlie said.

Welcome back, self-consciousness; it was a nice few seconds. "Thanks." It was a simple blue shift dress. I had also left my hair down. "Do you want to come in and relax for a bit or are you ready to turn right around?"

"Let's go now," he said. "If you're ready."

I nodded and climbed into his car. It reminded me of the 4th of July when he had driven me around all day. Naturally my mind stayed on the last ride, the uncomfortable one before we talked everything out, and that made me uncomfortable again. I was happy to see him, but I didn't want to say I was happy to see him for fear he'd take it the wrong way. My body would not relax and despite the thorough air conditioning, I felt warm all over.

"Do you mind some music?" Charlie asked.

"No, whatever you like."

He flipped on a country station. Not my first choice, but I still didn't mind.

Chapter 18

Riverwoods had a large side lawn with a large garden. I thought Andrew would like that. The building was brick and two stories high. Charlie and I went in the front entrance and walked up to a reception area. He introduced us and said he had called about getting a tour.

The red-headed woman behind the desk nodded. "Let me give Mary a call. She's expecting you so I'm sure she'll be down in a minute if you'd like to have a seat over there." The woman gestured to a long bench by the wall.

I assumed that Mary was a staff member. The woman who approached us was wearing a fluffy pink robe and pushing a walker. Her head was covered with tight gray curls. Her face was lined with age and alive with affability. "You young'uns here for the tour?" she asked.

"Yes, ma'am," Charlie said and we both stood.

"A body could get whiplash watching the pair of you stand so quickly. You make sure you don't leave me behind, you hear?"

"We don't know where we're going," I said.

"Right you are. I guess I do have an advantage. I'm Mary and I'll be your guide. And you are?"

She was looking at me so I said, "Rebecca. And this is Charlie."

"You two brother and sister?"

I shook my head.

"In that case," she said, "you're a lucky gal. He's a real cutie pie."

I laughed and Charlie turned away, probably trying to hide the fact that he was turning red. His ears gave him away.

"Okay, Mary," I said. "Where are you going to take us first?"

"Back to my place of course. Are you sure you have to come?" She glanced at Charlie and then winked at me.

"Lead the way," I told her.

"Right this way." Mary turned and took us down a hallway to our left. We passed a table where two older women were working on a jigsaw puzzle. One of them was wearing the thickest glasses I'd ever seen. Some of the rooms we passed had their doors open. I tried to keep my eyes forward anyway. It didn't feel right to look into the homes of strangers even if they seemed to be inviting me to do so. Mary's door was open, too, and she took us right inside.

I didn't realize until I walked in that I had been expecting something like a hospital room. It looked more like a small apartment though. The room we entered was a combination kitchen and living room and I could see a bed through an open door to the right.

"This here's the kitchen," Mary said. "The fridge has an icemaker that's real quiet. There's only two burners on the stove so I'm not making any Thanksgiving dinners in here, but it generally gets the job done. Some of us prefer to eat in the big dining room anyway." Mary was a thorough guide. She proceeded to show us the inside of each of her kitchen cabinets and even turned on the faucet to prove that water would come out.

"Then this here's the living room," she said as she made her way across the floor. "All the furniture is mine so you'd have to picture... uh, who are y'all looking at this place for anyway?"

"My grandpa," Charlie said.

"So you'd have to picture his things filling up the area."

Charlie and I looked around for a moment. I tried to picture the room with a few more doilies.

Mary said, "We could use a few more gentlemen in here. What do you think the odds are that he'll be moving in?"

"I believe my mom already has all the paperwork taken care of for him to move in early next week. I wanted to see the place for myself so I can tell him about it."

Mary nodded thoughtfully. "This grandfather of yours, is he a good God-fearing man?"

Charlie sort of shrugged and nodded.

"And do you get your looks from him?"

"I, uh..." Charlie didn't seem to have any idea what to say to that so Mary turned her questioning eyes past him to me.

I was glad I was behind Charlie so I could nod approvingly without him seeing. Mary gave me a thumbs-up and Charlie turned around and gave me a look I couldn't interpret. I returned an innocent smile.

Charlie hung back a bit while Mary showed me the bedroom and bathroom. There was a call button in each room in case the resident needed a nurse, but it otherwise felt like a regular apartment. It even had a small private patio. Mary was about to take us to see the rest of the facility when I was struck with an idea. "Mary," I said, "would you mind if I took a few pictures of the room to show Andrew?"

"Go ahead, honey. You can take one of me, too. That way he'll have a familiar face to look for."

I took out my phone and snapped a few photos. I got one of Mary and then one of Charlie while I was at it. She led us back past the reception area and to a dining room. I snapped another picture at the doorway. The room had about a dozen big round tables and a cafeteria-style kitchen at the back that appeared closed. It was very quiet, which was not surprising since we were in between regular meal times. The only other people in the room were three women sitting together at one of the tables and one of those women called out, "Hey, Mary, who've you got with you?"

Mary ushered us to the table. "This here is Charlie and, um, I'm sorry, hon… what's your name again?"

"Rebecca," I said to Mary, loud enough that they would all hear.

"That's right," Mary said. "Charlie's grandfather is going to be moving in soon. Won't that be a treat?"

One of the women tutted something about Mary and her constant talk of adding men to the residents. Another one asked, "Does he play Gin?"

Charlie and I both nodded. Sometimes Andrew talked us into playing with him on Sundays.

"Excellent," she said. "Why don't you kids sit and chat with us for a while?" The woman gestured to some open chairs.

"We don't want to intrude," I said.

"Nonsense. We love visitors. Why do you think we're in here instead of holed up in our rooms like some folks?"

I glanced at Charlie. He seemed a bit hesitant, but I thought we might get some inside scoop on the place. As we sat, the ladies introduced themselves and started right in on everything Andrew would need to know without me having to ask. They weren't the types to hold back on opinions and they let us know which foods in the dining room were edible and which ones they'd rather see used as fertilizer. They told us about which residents would talk your ear off and which would pretend to be deaf. I wasn't going to remember and didn't know who they were talking about anyway.

Charlie's phone rang at one point and he excused himself to take the call. The woman closest to me, and the one who had been doing most of the talking while the others nodded a lot, reached across the

93

table and seized my left hand. "I don't see a ring here," she said. "What's the story with you and him?"

I had to bite my tongue to keep in my first answer, which would not have been very respectful. Now even complete strangers wanted to know what was happening in my life. "There's no story," I said. "We haven't known each other that long."

"I think he knows everything he needs to." The woman turned to her friends and they exchanged knowing looks and more nods. Against my better judgment I asked, "What are you talking about?"

Mary said, "Haven't you noticed how we're all having a pleasant chat and Charlie hasn't said a word? He's too busy looking at you."

A woman with glasses on a beaded chain around her neck shook her head and said, "It's been a long time since I've seen a boy so lovesick."

I felt my face getting a bit hot. Mary said, "Oh, let's leave her alone now. We don't want to risk our invitations to the wedding."

Charlie returned, approaching the table slowly. I don't know if it was my red face or the laughter around me that made him cautious.

Instead of reclaiming his seat, he looked between me and Mary for a moment before he asked, "Well, Mary, is there more to the tour?"

"You know, I plumb forgot we were on a tour." She turned to grab her walker and Charlie held it steady for her. She rose slowly as she said, "Thanks for the chat, ladies. I have to return to my duties now."

Mary took us to a game room next. There was a schedule on the wall that showed the games for each night. She explained that Bingo usually had the biggest crowd, that Bridge was only for serious players, and a few other tidbits.

When we went back into the hallway, the women with the puzzle were admiring their work. I asked if they would mind posing with the finished project. Charlie said, "Haven't you taken enough pictures yet?"

I turned my phone on him as an answer.

"Did you just take a picture of me?"

"Yes," I said as I looked at my screen. "I think it's my favorite one of the day."

"Don't do that," Charlie said.

"Don't take pictures of you?"

He shook his head. Instead of clarifying, he looked at Mary who was looking at us. She continued the tour in something called the family room. It was a large room with several couches and a shelf of kid toys and games. Residents could reserve the room if they had too many visitors for their own rooms. Mary said the room was especially good for the "great-grands."

She took us back to the hallway and started listing the names of a few more people we'd have to meet. I caught Charlie's eye and he gave me a look that was not difficult to read. He asked if I was as ready to go as he was. I gave him a little nod.

He thanked Mary for showing us around and said that we had to get going. She made us promise to stop in to see her once we got Andrew settled.

"Hang on a second," I said to Charlie when we got outside. "I just want to get one of the garden." I took out the camera again and he waited patiently while I stretched the definition of one. Then we got back in his car. It had become an oven while we were inside.

"I'm sorry," he said. "I should have thought to cool this off for you."

"It'll only take a few minutes. You forget that I'm used to being hot."

"I don't forget." His tone suggested that he was not talking about my non-air conditioned house. He seemed to be talking to himself. I assumed that meant he didn't expect me to answer.

Instead I said, "What did you think of the tour?"

"Well..." Charlie started to slowly shake his head. "The rooms look pretty good and it's nice that they have games and stuff... but I feel bad about sending Grandpa someplace where he'll be so outnumbered."

"Oh, you mean all the women?"

"Yes, I mean all the women. Did you see a single other guy there?"

"Um..." I had to think about that. "I did actually. We didn't talk to him, but I saw a guy inside one of the rooms with an open door."

"Was he cowering in a corner?"

That made me laugh. "Don't worry. I think your grandpa will do just fine. He's not exactly shy about expressing opinions. He'll very politely let them know if they're bothering him."

Charlie just continued to shake his head. Honestly, I didn't entirely blame him. If the roles had been reversed I'm not sure I'd be excited about sending my grandma, or in my case my mom, somewhere she'd be a novelty. We would just have to work out a good visit schedule. I

95

turned my mind to more immediate concerns in the meantime. "Is your aunt and/or grandfather expecting you back at a certain time?"

"Not for a while. Actually, that call I got while we were in the dining room, that was my aunt. She said that her kids had decided to pick them up and take them to dinner. She said they probably wouldn't be back until at least seven or so. That means I'm on my own for dinner."

"We're going to make it back to Hartford by four. Can't you go with them?"

"She asked if I wanted to. She actually invited both of us, but I didn't think either of us wanted to drive right back to the city. Did you want to go with them?"

"No, it sounds like a family thing. Would you like to stay at my house and eat apples?"

"Seriously? You're eating just apples for dinner?"

"I cut them up and melt peanut butter on top. It's delicious."

"But that's a snack. Not a meal."

"I also have popcorn."

Charlie rolled his eyes at the road. "Oh, well, now that's a meal."

Chapter 19

"You're not a vegetarian, are you?" Charlie asked.

"Haven't I been eating meat in front of you every Sunday?"

"Are you just doing that to be nice?"

"No, I'd have said something by now if I didn't want to eat meat."

Charlie closed my refrigerator. "Then why is there never any meat in your house? You seem to only ever have fruits and vegetables."

"You're forgetting about all the baked goodies I've been having with Andrew. I need to eat a lot of healthy stuff to balance it out. Fruits and veggies are easy anyway because you can eat them raw. Meat requires cooking and cleaning up after the cooking. It doesn't seem worth the effort for one person."

Charlie smiled at me. "You need a grill."

"Not when I have you to grill for me."

That seemed to have been the wrong thing to say. Charlie quietly sat at the table where I had just put out two plates of apples cut up with peanut butter. I inadvertently reminded both of us that he was going to stop spending weekends with his grandfather and his grandfather's grill and possibly me. I had agreed to let him know if I wanted our relationship to change. I wasn't sure if I was doing something wrong by not saying that I wanted us to stay friends. I couldn't bring myself to do it though. I was so afraid he'd stop spending time with me. I sort of wished I could read his mind as he sat there crunching apples. I should have known he wasn't thinking about me at all. He was still thinking about meat.

"I don't think Grandpa will be able to take his grill with him. Do you think we could keep it in your garage so I could grill over here?"

I nodded. "Sure. Someday I'm going to have to clean out that garage, too. But I'm thinking that's a project for next summer."

"Have you decided on a date for the yard sale yet?"

"I'm thinking August 9th. That's three weeks away so you can spend next weekend helping your grandpa pack and the next weekend making sure he's settled. Then you can help me."

Charlie looked amused. "You've planned out my free time very well, haven't you?"

"Oh, I'm sorry. You said you wanted to help with the yard sale. But Aiden is bringing three friends so we can probably manage without you."

"I was only teasing. Of course I'm going to help. I'm curious which things will sell. Make sure you let Mabel know the date. Best advertising you can get."

When Charlie had to go, I walked him to the door and there was a moment of awkwardness. I think it was just me. I couldn't figure out what I was waiting for when I stood there with my hand on the knob not opening the door. After he left, I went through all the pictures I had taken at Riverwoods. I thought Andrew might appreciate looking at them the old fashioned way so I picked out my favorites and planned to stop after church to have them printed. I had seen a small empty album in one of those boxes upstairs and it only took me an hour to find it again. I could really tell that my house was becoming organized.

Andrew thanked me for showing him the pictures. I can't say that he was anything like excited about moving. He did seem determined to make the best of it though. When Charlie told him that he might regularly be the only man around, Andrew said that at least he'd be the best looking man around.

Charlie made hamburgers again. He seemed to have fun just watching them cook. While we ate, Charlie asked about one of the cousins who had taken Andrew out to dinner the previous night. Andrew couldn't remember when he had last seen him.

The evening otherwise went well and Charlie walked me home. It was still hot and sticky and bright so walking me home felt as unnecessarily formal as ever. But I liked prolonging the goodbye. I wouldn't see Charlie again until Saturday and I might not see much of him then. Several of his relatives were coming to help pack up Andrew's house. They were eventually going to sell it. I was going to stay out of the way.

Charlie thanked me again for checking out Riverwoods with him and said goodnight where the sidewalk turned to my house. When I got to the door, he was still standing on the corner. I took a picture of him as he waved. I didn't know what made me do that.

I ran to town Monday morning. On an impulse, I bought a can of tuna for a sandwich. It was the only meat I could think of that didn't require cooking. I told Mabel the date for my yard sale and confirmed the next time Aiden would be coming to mow my lawn. I had already talked to him about it directly, but I liked steering the topic when I talked to Mabel so she didn't bring up Charlie. On the way home I realized that I forgot to buy bread.

I went out to the garage in the afternoon to make sure there was room for a grill. I otherwise continued my resolve to ignore the garage. After dinner I called Sofia, the friend who had reached out to me a few weeks earlier. She sounded very happy with her new husband and much less happy with her new job. I was glad I called. I didn't tell her that I had done so because after a half hour of holding my phone I needed something to get my mind off calling Charlie.

I still couldn't seem to put the phone down so I looked through my pictures. That close-up of Charlie was still my favorite. I really liked the one of Mary, too. Her eyes were turned slightly to her right where I knew Charlie had been standing. I would definitely need to visit her again. Some of the garden pictures were nice but I liked the ones with people better.

Finally I just turned on the TV for a while and then decided to go to bed early. It was only a little after 9 p.m. when I switched off the TV. As I stood up and stretched, I had the strangest sensation that I wasn't alone. It wasn't a scary feeling. I hadn't seen or heard anything, yet I somehow knew that it was Andrew waiting on the other side of the stairway door.

I unlocked it to let him in. I had so far been careful not to let him know that I kept the interior door locked. He didn't say anything about that and I didn't say anything about how it was weird for him to come over at night. He walked in and said, "Good evening, Rebecca."

"Hi," I said. That was all. I was nearly speechless at the fact that he remembered my name.

"I can't stay long. I just had a few things to tell you."

"Okay."

"You're so much like Rose. We thought you should look in the bible. You've been struggling a bit and it's always good for young people to figure things out for themselves, but," he stopped and winked at me, "a little hint won't hurt."

He seemed to think he was giving me some valuable advice. But I already knew the bible contained some good information and he wasn't even narrowing it down to a specific book. He continued without waiting for me to respond.

99

"The other thing is that I know you'll be good for my Charlie. I'm happy we've gotten to know each other and sorry that I have to leave."

"Andrew, you know Riverwoods isn't that far. I'm going to visit you all the time."

He smiled at me. "You're a good girl. Walk me out?"

"You're going already?"

"I've said what I needed to." He moved towards the front door. I followed and opened it for him. "Goodnight, Rebecca."

"Goodnight, Andrew."

I pulled out my bible before bed. I didn't know what Andrew wanted me to read. If he asked though, I wanted to be able to say I tried to follow his advice. I let it fall open in front of me and with my eyes closed I dropped a finger onto a page. It landed somewhere in I Corinthians. "If anyone supposes he knows something, he does not yet know as he ought to know."

That was great. I did not appreciate the reminder that I didn't know anything. I suspect God did not appreciate the sarcasm in my reply. I couldn't help it. I closed my eyes and made a mental note to buy bread in the morning.

It rained overnight so I put on an older pair of running shoes in case I found some puddles on my way to town. I was about to pick up my backpack when I heard my phone ringing from the pocket. It was Charlie.

"Rebecca? I'm glad I caught you before your run."

He didn't sound glad. I could tell by the shake in his voice that something was wrong. "Charlie? What's going on?"

"I thought you'd want to know. Grandpa... he passed away."

There was a strange tightening in my chest. "What happened?" I asked.

"I don't know. My mom was there. She said he told her last night that he wasn't feeling well and was going to bed early. Then he just never woke up. We don't know when exactly..."

"I'm so sorry," I said. I thought Charlie might be crying and I wished he was closer.

"Aunt Margaret is with my mom and dad and they're working on, you know, arrangements and stuff. Do you want me to call you back when I know when the funeral will be?"

It sounded as though Charlie was trying to get off the phone. "Okay. Or you can just text me a time. But I'll talk to you soon I hope."

100

I put the phone back in its pocket and messed with the flap. It was crooked as I closed it and reclosed it. I couldn't seem to get it to lie flat. Eventually I gave up and put the backpack on. The run started out fine, but for some reason the music was bothering me so I pulled out the earbuds and stuffed them in my pocket.

When I got to the store I couldn't remember what I was going to buy. I picked up some bananas because I liked bananas. They were probably the easiest fruit to eat. No washing or cutting required. Bread. That was the other thing I needed. I found a small package with a plastic insert that would keep it from getting terribly squashed in my backpack. I tried to remember if there was anything else I wanted to buy and all I could think about was tea. It didn't make any sense since Andrew wasn't going to come over and drink it for me. But I knew at that moment that I *needed* tea.

I went up front and smiled at Mabel.

"Morning, hon. Did you hear the sad news today? Andrew Lately passed."

I nodded. "Charlie called me."

"They were tight," she said. "It's good he'll have you to lean on."

I nodded again. I didn't really think there was anything I could do for Charlie though.

"And the Kelleys had a new baby yesterday. Can you believe that? It makes five for them."

"That's nice. Mom and baby are doing well?" I asked.

"As far as I know. I hear he was a nine-pounder."

I didn't know enough about babies to know if I should look shocked or just surprised so I tried to mirror Mabel's expression. "Have a good day," I said as I left.

I didn't need any more calligraphy supplies so I started for home. I couldn't get the right pace though. First I was moving too fast. My parents power walk, but I've never gotten into it. Then I seemed to be plodding. I broke into a run. That felt better. I needed to run. I ran right past my house. I saw an unfamiliar car in Andrew's driveway and turned around quickly. I kept running all the way back to my house.

I stayed in the shower until the water started to get cold. I got dressed before I realized that I had forgotten to unload my groceries. I pulled out the tea first. It was really stupid to buy something I didn't like. I threw the whole box into the trash unopened. Then I went to the cupboard and grabbed a few bags of tea left from another box. I tossed those as well. I picked up the teapot with the strawberries on

101

the sides. I still thought it was the prettiest one and I never got to use it because it still didn't have cups that matched. I put the teapot on top of the trash can and pushed down hard. It didn't fit. I opened the back door and hurled the useless thing onto the sidewalk. I didn't care that I'd have to clean up the shattered bits later.

I sat in the living room with a book. It was a thriller and the words were not holding my attention. My eyes kept moving to that dull circle I had left on the coffee table with my first cup of disgusting tea. I tried to put my feet on the table to cover it. That was uncomfortable. I dropped my book over the spot and left it splayed with the cover bent.

I went into my bedroom to watch TV. I had my phone nearby in case Charlie called. He texted me in the afternoon with a time and place for the visitation. It would be Thursday evening and the funeral the following morning. He asked if I could come to both. I replied that I would. Then I called my parents. They knew Andrew a little and I thought they'd want to know he died. I also wanted to ask a favor. My mom answered.

"Hi, Mom. It's Rebecca."

"No one else calls me Mom," she said. She always said that. She was also the same person who taught me to identify myself on the phone.

"How are you, Mom?"

"The usual. Is anything new with you, honey?"

"Sort of. I was calling... I wondered if you'd heard... Andrew Lately died last night."

"Oh, no! I'm so sorry. The two of you had been spending so much time together. Are you okay?"

"I'm fine, Mom. It's not like I really knew him all that long."

"Are you sure? Do you want me to come over?"

"No, really, I'm fine."

I could hear voices as she pulled the phone away. My dad had obviously asked what had happened and she was filling him in. I heard a click as my dad picked up another phone. My parents didn't do speaker phone. "Rebecca," he said, "I'm sorry to hear about Andrew. Has the funeral been scheduled yet?"

"Friday morning at 10:30. I think I'm going to the visitation, too. I wondered if I could stay the night Thursday."

"Of course, honey," my mom said. "Your old room is just as you left it."

"You didn't turn it into a study the day after I left?" I hadn't been back to the house since I moved out. I thought I showed a bit of maturity by saying "since I left" instead of "since you kicked me out."

My dad said, "A guest room never hurts."

Even though my mom tried to cover the phone, I heard her add, "Or a place for grandkids."

My mom had been talking about grandkids forever. I had been ignoring her forever. For the first time, it occurred to me that I might not have forever to make that dream come true. "Well, anyway," I said, "I just wanted to make sure the room was available. I'll be there sometime Thursday evening."

"Okay, honey. You let us know if you need anything between now and then."

Chapter 20

The next two days were something of a blur. I spent a lot of time giving my house the most thorough cleaning I could manage and I still couldn't get that spot off the coffee table. Twice I got in my car and thought about driving to the city and twice I went back into the house when I couldn't think of an excuse.

I thought I would have trouble deciding what to wear on Thursday evening. I forgot how generous Andrew was with compliments though. As soon as I opened my closet I found a deep purple dress he had said he liked. It was sleeveless, but had a matching sweater. It would be perfect for the air conditioned funeral home. I found a blue one he liked, too, and packed that one for Friday morning. I bought the paper with his obituary. It was on my kitchen table. I hadn't figured out what to do with it other than not put it in the recycling bin.

The visitation started at 6 p.m. and lasted two hours. I planned to drive into the city early and get something to eat nearby so I could show up right at 6 o'clock. I knew it was a drop-in thing where punctuality wasn't necessary, but it felt necessary. I hadn't heard from Charlie since he texted me the address of the funeral home. I wanted to call and see how he was doing, but I didn't want to intrude if he was busy with family. I knew from Mabel that Andrew's brother William was flying in and I assumed other family would be gathering as well. Charlie had specifically asked me to come to the visitation though. That was the one thing he wanted me to do so I was going to get there as soon as I could.

About a dozen people were in the room when I entered. It was a large room and everyone was spread out. I was able to spot Charlie right away standing next to a window with thick burgundy drapes. He was wearing a tie. It made him look older, which made him look closer to his actual age. He smiled when he saw me and I don't think I imagined that he looked relieved. Coming at the start was the right decision.

I walked up and hugged him. I wasn't a big hugger and I didn't think he was either, but it seemed appropriate. I held on for a few

104

seconds because I had missed him. He whispered, "Thank you for coming," in my ear. I nodded into his shoulder. Then he let go and introduced me to the men next to us. One was his dad and the other was his uncle.

His dad said, "A lot of people here are going to want to meet you. And here comes one of them now."

I turned to follow his gaze and saw a woman walking towards us. She had straight hair touching her shoulders that was a mix of brown and gray. She wore a navy sweater over a long paisley skirt. I was pretty sure she was Charlie's mom.

"Are you Rebecca?" she asked and put her hand out to me.

"Yes," I said. "Rebecca Hilson."

She gave my hand more of a squeeze than a shake. "I'm Michelle Tate. I wanted to make sure I thanked you for being so kind to Dad this summer. He loved having someone new to tell his stories to."

"I enjoyed hearing the stories."

"I think some had gotten embellished over the years. But they were definitely entertaining." I got the impression that she had more to say to me, but she was interrupted by a middle-aged couple wanting to offer condolences. Charlie and I moved off to the side.

I asked him how he was doing.

"Not too bad really," he said. "I think I've gotten over the shock. It was hard to see him when he was confused or too forgetful. I guess that makes this, I don't know, not as bad as it might have been."

I thought I knew what he meant. Death was never easy. Sometimes it made more sense than others. The overall mood was serious, not depressing. Most people seemed to agree it was good that Andrew was able to go while he was still in his own home. I'm not sure if I stayed next to Charlie or if he stayed next to me. But he was always right there as I met one relative after another. William looked a lot like Andrew except with a pale gray beard. I saw Charlie's sister and brother-in-law again. They didn't have the toddler with them. His youngest sister had red-rimmed eyes, but she told me I could do better than her "doofus brother" so there were some holes in her grief.

Margaret came up and introduced me to her husband and thanked me for coming.

"I'm sorry for your loss," I said. It still sounded lame. There was nothing better to say though.

She nodded. "Dad was so fond of you. You know, he told me just last week that even though you were technically his niece, you felt more like a granddaughter. Even when he was confused, he knew you felt like family." She smiled and then winked at Charlie. "And maybe someday you really will be family."

I tried to smile benignly. It was not the time to dash anyone's hopes. Margaret moved away to greet a woman I recognized from the church. My parents showed up, too. They asked how I was and chatted with William for a while. They didn't stay long. There was a lot of coming and going. I saw Mabel briefly. I wondered how long Charlie expected me to stay.

"Do you want me to stay longer?" I asked him in a moment when we were alone.

"Are you getting tired?"

This wasn't about me. "Do you want me to stay?" I repeated.

He nodded. "I like introducing you to everyone. It gives me something to say."

"I'll stay then. I need to find a restroom though, and then I'll come right back. Okay?"

"It's out that door and to the left," he said.

I followed his directions. When I came back, he hadn't moved. He was talking to a young man I hadn't met yet. Charlie's mom grabbed me before I could get across the room. "Rebecca," she said, "thank you again for coming. I know it's helping Charlie."

"I wanted to be here. Andrew was a good man."

"Thank you. We're going to have to have you over sometime to get to know you better. We should have done it before, but we've been rather wrapped up in trying to look after Dad."

"I think I'd like that," I said. I was trying to be polite and not let her know that I was cringing on the inside. It was making me uncomfortable that all of Charlie's family believed we were a couple. I bore some responsibility for that by leaving things ambiguous.

Charlie's mom smiled at me. "We've been seeing so much more of his dent since he met you."

"His dent?"

"On his cheek. Did he tell you how he got that?"

I shook my head. I had assumed he was born with it.

"He ran into the corner of a table when he was a toddler. It left a horrible bruise all over the side of his face. When it cleared up, there was this little dent like a man-made dimple that shows up when he smiles. I think I expected it to go away for at least a year. Now I'm kind of glad it didn't. I think it's so cute."

106

"So do I," I said. Out loud. I hadn't meant to say it out loud.

Charlie's mom beamed. Soon she was going to hate me. I had let things go on too long. Charlie was going to get hurt and this woman smiling at me was going to hate me for it. "Go on back," she said. "I can tell he's waiting to introduce you to Patrick."

Charlie and the other guy, presumably named Patrick, were both looking at us. I went back to Charlie and learned that Patrick was one of his best friends, a former college roommate. I had heard a few things about Patrick and was glad to put a face with the name. Soon after that I met a few people who worked with Charlie. They came in together and left quickly. Then things began to quiet down.

I had met all the family that was there and no one new came during the last half hour or so. Charlie and I ended up in a corner by ourselves. "I'm sorry if this was too much for you," he said.

"It was only too much if you expect me to remember everyone's name."

"Are you sure? You look kind of tired."

I wasn't surprised that I looked tired. I had gotten very little sleep the last two nights. "I'm fine," I assured him. "I'm staying with my parents tonight so I don't have to drive to Hartford and then back in the morning."

"Will you come and find me at the church?"

"Find you?"

"Yeah, I'll be up front with the family. Will you come and sit with me?"

"If you want me to."

"Thanks. While I'm asking favors..." Charlie hesitated.

So far he hadn't asked that much of me. "Go ahead," I prompted.

"Well, a bunch of us are going to spend Saturday at Grandpa's house. We were already planning to gather to help him pack so we thought we might as well start going through the stuff in his house. I don't think it's going to be anywhere near as much fun as helping you clean out your house." He stopped and sighed. There seemed to be a big mix of emotions in that sigh. "And I hoped maybe you'd let me come over for a break sometime. Maybe in the evening so I'll have something to look forward to?"

That was a favor? "Do you want to have dinner with me? I'll get a pizza. Fruits and vegetables are great, but not comfort food. I think you need comfort food."

That cute dent showed up just a fraction of a second before the rest of his smile. "Comfort food and a box of mystery supplies?" he asked hopefully.

"Yes. I think that's exactly what you need."

Charlie's sister came over to say goodnight. They were going home to relieve the babysitter. It was nearly 8 o'clock and everyone was gathering their belongings and making sure they all knew who was riding with whom in the morning. I stole a peek at Andrew in the casket. He was still on the far side of the room. Charlie surprised me with another hug. His warmth made something in the back of my throat hurt terribly before I let go. "See you tomorrow," he said.

I swallowed hard as I turned to leave.

My parents were sitting in the living room when I came in with my overnight bag. I sort of forgot that I should knock now that I didn't live there. Dad switched off the TV and Mom rushed over to me. "How are you holding up, honey?"

"I'm fine, Mom. Just tired. I'm going to get ready for bed early and maybe just read in my room for a bit."

Dad nodded and said, "Goodnight."

Mom looked like she was going to hug me. We were not a hugging family so I took a step backward and said, "Mom, I said I'm fine."

She said, "You don't look… okay, goodnight then."

My room really was exactly as I had left it. It felt as though I'd been away for years though. I lay in bed and tried to pray. I couldn't think of anything to say and it was early so I pulled out a rosary. I did like the way the beads gave me something to hold while I prayed. Something tangible was good when God felt far away. When I closed my eyes for the night, I thought about how I didn't need to make a shopping list. My mom would have a well-stocked kitchen waiting for me. She might even make pancakes. It would be a nice change. I realized though that I didn't miss it. I mostly enjoyed the life I was carving out for myself. Or I had enjoyed it. I wouldn't let myself think of my Sundays with Andrew and Charlie. I didn't want to think about anything. I just wanted to sleep. I tossed and turned all night thinking about how much I wanted to sleep.

Chapter 21

My parents were going to the funeral and asked if I wanted to ride with them. I believe they were trying to make sure I came back with them so we could talk for a while. I wanted to take my car so I could go home when it was over. I promised them that we'd have more time to talk at Sunday lunch.

The church felt different when I entered. My aunt's funeral had been there, too. I remembered where I sat then and went up to see if Charlie was there. He was watching for me. He was wearing a black suit and looked really nice. I kicked myself for noticing that at such an inappropriate time.

I took the seat next to him and he leaned over and whispered. "Hi. You look great."

We sat quietly as the service started. Andrew had been a member of the Knights of Columbus. The other members were there in their fluffy hats and capes. It was nice. I thought Andrew's farewell could use a little pomp. I looked over at Charlie next to me. If my heart could break, the expression on his face would have done it. He wasn't crying. His eyes looked glassy and he was staring at the backs of his hands on his lap. In that moment it didn't matter whether our relationship had an official status or not. It only mattered that I thought I could provide some small measure of comfort. I slipped my hand under his. He closed his eyes and held on like he never wanted to let go.

That was when something I didn't even know I was fighting finally won. Hot tears fell down my face as though poured from a steaming tea kettle. I could barely breathe through the burning in my throat and I wanted to run. I couldn't bear to be still. But Charlie was still gripping my hand and I couldn't cause a scene. Someone passed him a few tissues and he gave them to me. It was his mom and I was so embarrassed. It was her father in the coffin. She shouldn't be passing tissues to someone who had only known him a short time.

Charlie let go of my hand and put his arm around me. That was worse. I was supposed to be there for him. I shook with the effort of keeping my sobs silent. There wasn't anything I could do so I eventually gave up and relaxed into Charlie's side. The tears slowed as soon as I stopped fighting them. I concentrated on breathing calmly. When the episode passed, he took my hand again and I let him keep it until the end. It felt very natural and not exactly friendly. I really hoped I wasn't further complicating things between us.

I don't remember much of what happened at the cemetery. I know that Charlie's Aunt Margaret invited me to her house afterward. She said that was where the family was gathering. Charlie answered for me, insisted that I needed to go home and rest. I didn't argue. When I got home I went into the bedroom to change clothes and lay down on my bed instead. It was late in the evening by the time I woke up.

I wandered into the kitchen for a snack since I hadn't had lunch or dinner. At the table I munched crackers with one hand and flipped through pictures on my phone with the other. The only one I had of Andrew was him looking at the pictures I took of Riverwoods. Charlie was in the background fixing the doily that had evidently fallen off the chair and onto his shoulder. I hadn't noticed that before. I stared at the picture while I thought about Andrew. I wasn't afraid to think about him now that I was all cried out. I remembered how he scared me that first day. It occurred to me that I might have scared him just as badly by dropping that heavy shovel. Then I thought about the last time he came to see me. Several thoughts came together all at once to create a very eerie possibility in my mind.

I remembered how I knew he was there without hearing him come in or knock. I remembered how clear-headed he was, even knowing my name for what I was sure was the first time. And Charlie's mom had said that Andrew went to bed early the night he died. She hadn't mentioned him leaving the house.

Had he known it was the end and snuck out to see me or had he actually visited me after... after...

The message I had dismissed as unhelpful suddenly seemed very important. I got out a piece of paper and worked to remember his exact words. "We think you should look in the bible."

Who was we? He had said I was like Rose. Andrew and Rose thought I should look in the bible? I still didn't understand. I went to my room and picked up my bible. What was I supposed to see? There was so much information inside. My eyes fell on the nightstand and possible understanding came to me. Maybe they had meant a specific bible, Rose's family bible.

I pulled the big heavy thing out of the drawer. There on the first page was the list of births and deaths. I noticed that Rose's death hadn't been recorded. Something told me that wasn't what I needed to see, but I found a pen and put in the date anyway. Then I turned the page and gasped.

There was a small note tucked between the pages and the envelope had my name on it! Rose had left me a note. Why was it here and not with her will? I picked it up carefully, cautiously. The page it was lying on was a record of marriages. I instinctively scanned to the bottom to find my parents. I knew they were the last marriage in the family. But I was wrong about what I knew. Beneath my parents it said, "Rose Hilson to Andrew Lately – May 30th 2001."

I was no longer afraid of the letter, but very, very curious. I opened it up as quickly as I could without tearing it.

> *Dear Rebecca,*
>
> *I thought I should explain in case you stumble across this record of my marriage. Andrew and I married soon after Martha passed and folks in town sure love their gossip. We were afraid the fact that we were teenage sweethearts might cause unwanted speculation. Andrew is an honorable man who loves with his whole heart. There was no room for me while Martha was alive. I do not feel the need to clarify that with anyone outside the family.*
>
> *Our plan was to tell the families after some time had passed. But as time did pass, we became concerned that feelings would be hurt for having been excluded or that it would appear there had been something to hide. It seemed best to keep it a secret. There is no marriage license. And we went outside the Church to have it kept secret, another reason we were afraid the families might be upset.*
>
> *I am truly sorry if this news causes any pain. We could do only what felt right at the time.*
>
> *God Bless,*
> *Rose*

I wasn't sure how my dad would feel about this and at the moment I wasn't sure I needed to tell him. But I thought it was wonderful. Andrew really was family.

I eagerly flipped through the bible to see if there were any other surprises. There were a lot of things tucked into its pages, mostly birth and death notices clipped from newspapers. I cut out Andrew's

111

obituary and put it with Rose's letter. There was something interesting in the middle of the book. It was an envelope addressed to Rose in handwriting I was sure matched the letters from Andrew in her journal. But this one was yellowed and the address faded. Inside the envelope was what appeared to be several letters and envelopes, all torn to tiny bits. I had no idea what had caused their relationship to end the first time, but Rose must have felt pretty strongly about it to have so thoroughly destroyed his letters and yet still saved them.

Of course she did.

A rush of regret came over me as I realized how incredibly unfair I had been to her memory, assuming she was cold and unfeeling just because she was reserved about showing her emotions. This was a woman who spent hours in the kitchen because people liked her cinnamon rolls. She scared the neighborhood kids because they wanted to be scared. Her journal was full of careful notes about which vegetables which neighbors enjoyed. Rose moved in with her mother to care for her during the last year of her life and she kept her own marriage a secret to protect the reputation of the man she loved. She loved deeply and privately.

And I was exactly like her. Just because I didn't wear my heart on my sleeve didn't mean I didn't have one. I had been trying to figure out why I had come so completely unglued at the funeral. Now I knew. I knew. I couldn't hide two emotions at once, grief *and* love. I kept my feelings over Andrew's death pushed far inside and when Charlie squeezed my hand there wasn't room for the love, too. I loved Charlie. It was both scary and wonderful to admit that to myself. I couldn't even imagine how terrifying it might be to admit it to Charlie. I wasn't ready for that. Charlie might not be ready for that either.

Saturday felt normal. Friday I went to a funeral, then came home and recognized that I was in love. It seemed that my life should have been completely shaken up by the emotional upheaval. But I still got up, ate cereal and put on my running shoes. I was still me, just a very slightly more mature version of me.

"Good morning, Mabel," I said as I put down my fruit.

"Morning, hon."

"Is Pops the only place in town to get pizza?" I asked her.

"No, but it's the best. Are you planning on splitting this pizza with someone I hear is helping pack up his grandpa's house today?"

This woman knew everything. I figured I might as well admit it. "Yes, I'm having dinner with Charlie."

"I knew you'd start confiding in me eventually. Things pretty serious between you two then?" She looked at me hopefully.

"Serious enough to share a pizza." I waved goodbye as I took my groceries. I was eager to see Jill.

"Rebecca," she called over the clanging, "how's the calligraphy working for you? I think you've been at it long enough to form an opinion."

"I stand by my original opinion. It was fun to try but now I'm kind of over it."

"Okay, I've been thinking about what you might want to try next and I have a few ideas."

"I think I might have an idea, too."

Jill put her arms up in celebration. "Wonderful! Let's hear it."

"Do you have any books on photography? Or just something that will help me pick out a good camera?"

"A camera? That's perfect! I can totally see you taking pictures. Let me help you."

"That's why I'm here."

"This way, this way," she said as she led me to a shelf of books near the back of her store. Her short pigtails bobbed as she practically skipped ahead of me. Jill was not the kind of person to keep emotions inside. We couldn't find exactly what I wanted or what she wanted for me. But she was still an excellent resource. She took me to her computer and pulled up her contact list. It was sorted by interest. She called two of the photographers on her list, one a professional and one an amateur. She asked them about cameras for beginners while constantly turning to me to relay information or ask more questions. She was like a hobby agent. After almost an hour, she had ordered what would be the perfect camera for me.

Chapter 22

Charlie called me in the afternoon to find out when he should come over. I asked him what he liked on his pizza and told him I'd let him know as soon as I was home with it. I texted him from my driveway and he was at my front door before I had plates and glasses on the table.

"That was fast," I said as I opened the door.

He pointed down the street. "Three houses away, remember?"

"That was still fast. You must be hungry."

"It smells good," he said.

We sat across from each other and began to eat. Smelling it in the car had made me pretty hungry, too.

"How are things going over there today?" I asked.

"Well, more work than I expected and not as depressing so I guess good and bad. Melissa is flying back to Maryland on Tuesday so she and my mom and Margaret decided that they wanted to have everything taken care of by then. First we went through the house looking for keepsakes. There were a few tense moments deciding who was going to keep what, but that mostly worked out. No one fought me on the grill." He paused and flashed a smile. "Since then we've mostly been shoving stuff into bags and boxes. Putting stuff into boxes is not nearly as much fun as looking through them was with you."

"Are you burned out on boxes in general or do you still want to find out what's in my last one tonight?"

Charlie tried to hide a slightly embarrassed smile. "Am I a huge geek if I say I've been looking forward to it all day?"

"I'm afraid so. But I've kind of been looking forward to it, too."

"Really?"

"I just get excited because you do. You know the proverbial kid in a candy store? That's you when we're about to open another box. We've mostly found useless stuff and yet… I don't know how you can still expect something interesting."

"It's not that I expect to find something good. It's that I don't know what we'll find. I guess I just like surprises."

"Speaking of surprises… I found an enormous one yesterday." I felt my grin stretch all the way across my face. I was thrilled to know of a secret marriage in a town where everyone probably now knew that I liked extra cheese on my pizza.

"What is it?" Charlie asked.

"I'm not telling. Not yet anyway."

Charlie picked up another slice and said, "I'll eat fast so we can get to the surprises."

His enthusiasm was so cute. I hoped he was as happy to be in on the secret as I was and didn't feel as though his grandmother had been slighted in any way.

The last box, marked "misc. supplies," was waiting for us in the living room. It was on the coffee table. Charlie got there first and sat down on the floor in front of it. He pulled the box down next to him and looked up at me. I was suddenly nervous as I found a piece of carpet for myself. I wondered if he remembered holding my hand in church. At the time I worried he might take it as a signal that our relationship had shifted. Now I worried that he hadn't. I didn't try to keep the box between us.

"How do you want to do this?" he asked.

I forced my mind onto the box and off of Charlie's knee, which was no more than two inches from bumping mine. "I can't just pull the lid off?" I asked. "Are you sure you want to prolong the moment you find out it's nothing but thousands of Q-tips?"

Charlie laughed at me. "Thousands of Q-tips? Is that seriously the most useless thing you could think of?"

"Well, I'm not the one who's been thinking about it all day."

"Okay, so here's what I think," he said. "I think we should take turns reaching in and pulling stuff out without looking."

"You want to reach into a completely unknown box blind?"

"It's not like there's going to be something alive in here."

"Eww."

"Eww what?"

"I'd rather find something alive than something dead."

"Stop trying to spoil the fun. Nothing in this box is or has ever been alive. It's not labeled miscellaneous pets."

Charlie was right. I was being silly on purpose, but so was he. Miscellaneous pets indeed. Then I thought of a real possibility. "What about sharp things?"

"We'll be careful."

"You go first," I said.

He turned his head away from the box, and towards me, while he slipped one hand under the lid. He immediately got this weird look on his face. Then he smiled and pulled out a fuzzy slipper. "It was really soft," he said. "And your talk of animals had me creeped out for a second."

"One slipper? Am I supposed to feel around and find the other one now?"

Charlie shook his head. "Maybe there is only one."

"Why would anyone save one slipper?"

"Why would anyone save a pickle jar full of seashells?"

"Good point."

"Your turn," Charlie nodded eagerly at the box. "Just pull out whatever you touch first."

"If I pull out something disgusting, I'm going to drop it on you."

"And I will deserve it. But I'm not worried." He motioned to the box to encourage me to try.

I looked away and put my hand under the lid. My hand touched something smooth. A book? No, it was another lid. A shoebox. "I think I found a shoebox," I said. "Should I pull out the whole thing?"

Charlie nodded.

"Hang on... I think I'm going to need both hands." I tried to get my other hand inside the box without knocking the lid off and without seeing inside. Charlie held the lid steady and I pulled out a shoebox. I took its lid off and couldn't help laughing. Inside the shoebox was a whole bunch of little boxes, sizes that jewelry might come in. "This might be a long turn," I said.

"That's okay, I like watching you."

I knew what he meant, that it was still fun for him when I was the one revealing things. But the comment made my ears a little warm. I started opening the tiny boxes to direct his attention to my hands. Most of the boxes did contain jewelry. I was reasonably sure that none of it was valuable, but some was pretty. I put aside a few things I intended to keep. The rest could go in the yard sale.

Charlie put his hand in the box. "Hmm," he said. "I found something smooth and hard. Wooden maybe? It's... ahh!"

116

We both jumped back and then laughed. We were startled by two loud chimes coming from inside the box. Charlie said, "I think I just lifted the lid on a music box."

I nodded. "Go ahead and get it out. I'm ready this time."

"Okay." Charlie put his hand back in the box and a song started playing as he pulled out a wooden music box by its open lid. It was a roughly four-inch cube with little umbrellas and rain boots carved into the sides. I recognized the tune as "Raindrops Keep Falling on My Head." With the lid open you could see the cylinder turning with its knobs picking out the song. Charlie watched it for a minute while the music played and I watched him. The music ended abruptly and he turned to me. "Do you want to keep this?"

"I don't know. It's cool, but I think I'd get sick of that song."

"Isaac can listen to the same thing over and over. I bet he'd love to watch this."

Isaac was Charlie's nephew. I said, "You should take it and give it to him then."

"Are you sure? I was just making an observation. I wasn't really suggesting what you should do with this."

"I'm sure. You should definitely give it to him."

Charlie showed me his dimple. "Okay, but only because he'll probably drive my sister insane with it."

I stuck my hand in the box and felt what must be the match for the slipper. When I got it out though, it did not match. The first slipper was navy and for a woman, mine was much smaller and pink. "I predict more slippers in our future," I said.

"I'll see if I can find one," Charlie said as he reached in. His hand came out with something else soft. It was a small teddy bear. It had a ribbon around its neck that had "Rebecca" printed on it. "Is this yours?" he asked.

"I don't remember it." I didn't wait for Charlie to say it was my turn. I was getting curious as to what else might be in the box. My hand touched something. It felt like an old VHS tape. I took it out and looked at it. There was no case. Someone had printed "Cinderella" on the label.

Charlie shrugged and reached into the box. He found another small pink slipper. Then my hand found something hard and unusually shaped. "I have no idea what this is." I pulled it out and said, "Oh!"

117

It was a shell-shaped nightlight. I was surprised that I hadn't recognized the feel of the prongs on the plug.

"Pictures!" Charlie said.

He had taken his turn while I was still examining the nightlight. There was something vaguely familiar about it. Now Charlie was holding a yellow photo envelope, fresh from a drug store. He smiled as he pulled out the first picture. "This is you, isn't it?"

He handed it to me and looked at the next one. I nodded as I took it. It was me. I looked about five years old. I was grinning from ear to ear and wearing most, if not all, of the jewelry we had found in the box. The next picture was Rose. She was holding up a ring-covered hand. The picture was crooked and part of her head hadn't made it into the shot. I had a feeling the kid in the first picture had taken the second one. There were several more of me wearing the jewelry and I seemed to be dancing in at least one. Then came a picture of me in a kitchen I didn't recognize with both of my hands squashed into a mound of what looked like bread dough. My face showed some serious concentration and it made the current me laugh. I probably looked exactly like that trying to follow her recipes now.

Then Charlie handed me a picture of me standing next to a car with my parents. I was waving. "I know what this is," I said. "My mom told me before that I had sleepovers with Aunt Rose when I was very little. That was before we moved to Atlanta and she had already moved in here to take care of her mom when we came back."

"You don't remember it though?"

I shook my head. It wasn't something I could help and yet I felt bad that the sleepovers hadn't left more of an impression on me. After a moment, I realized that wasn't the real reason for my regret. "I wish we had been closer," I said.

"Did you and your aunt not get along?"

"No, we did. We just didn't make time for each other. Here she was living 30 minutes away and well, the last ten years or so we came over here for Thanksgiving and she came to our house for Christmas. That was pretty much it. I know my parents talked to her on the phone sometimes, but... I've never been one to call people up to chat. If I don't have specific business, I mean... I guess I'd rather be face to face with someone."

I looked at Charlie. We were face to face. His eyes were on mine so intently that I was sure he was thinking about kissing me. I felt a rush of adrenaline as I thought about what was coming. He simply turned back to the photos he was still holding.

Had the sparks been my imagination? I had been so caught up in deciding how I felt about Charlie that I hadn't left time to consider how he might feel about me. Maybe he was glad we had decided to stay only friends.

"Well," he said, "if it makes you feel better I don't think she was lonely."

He could not have felt what I felt and gone right back to the conversation. I bit my lip and tried to remember what we had been talking about. "Who wasn't lonely?" I mumbled.

Charlie flashed a confused glance my direction. "Your aunt. I don't think anyone could be lonely in this town where everyone knows everyone. And Grandpa spent all kinds of time with her. In fact," he smiled to himself for a moment, "we used to wonder if something might happen between those two. You know, he proposed to my grandmother after only two weeks."

"Two weeks?" I repeated.

Charlie nodded. "Yeah, I guess it took her a few more weeks to actually say yes, but the man moved fast... then he spent something like twelve years just visiting Rose."

"Wait right here," I said as I jumped up. It felt like a good time to reveal what was written in our family bible. I went to my room and brought it out. "Do you remember when I said I found something surprising?"

"Of course. Is it time for you to tell me?"

I reclaimed my spot next to him with the heavy book on my lap. "This bible has some family records in it and I think you should see what it says." He looked over my shoulder while I flipped it to the second page. I pointed to the word "Marriages" before sliding my finger down to where it listed Rose and Andrew.

Charlie's eyes bugged out a little. "Is that real?" he asked.

"Yeah." I pointed to Rose's note. "She explained in here that they married fast. It was only a few months after your grandma died and they were afraid people would gossip, say there had been something going on before."

Charlie sighed. "Unfortunately, they were probably right about that."

119

"So they were just going to wait a while before they told people, but then they were afraid the family might be upset that they kept it a secret so they never told anyone."

Other than the apparent surprise, I wasn't sure how Charlie was taking the news. He was quietly processing it. Then he said, "He told me once."

"He did?"

"Not really. I mean, I thought he was kidding. It was that year in high school when I stayed with him. According to this they had already been married more than a year. I asked him about something, something that I guess Rose must have asked him to do and he said, 'Someday you'll learn you have to do what the wife wants.' I'm sure I just laughed and maybe even said something like, 'Rose isn't your wife.'" Charlie was smiling at the memory so I guessed he didn't feel betrayed at all.

"Do you think we should tell anyone else?" I asked.

A line appeared across Charlie's forehead while he considered it. "I'm not sure," he said. "I guess people don't really need to know and if there is a chance they'd feel..." He squinted at the date in the bible. "Wow, this was barely three months after Grandma died and he had to have..."

Charlie stopped talking abruptly and fixed me with a solemn look. "How in the world do you suppose he got two women to marry him in almost no time at all?"

I smiled at Charlie's astonishment. "I bet his love letters helped."

"Love letters?" Charlie pushed his eyebrows up and I winced with regret.

"I only read one before I knew what they were and before I realized it was written by someone I knew." I closed the bible and slid it over to the floor next to me. I figured the action would change the subject or revert it back to our box of supplies.

I heard Charlie take a deep breath before he said, "Do you want to get married?"

I didn't have time to react before he added, "I mean, in general. That wasn't supposed to sound like... I meant in general."

I said. "Yes, in general."

"You said before that someone asked you and you weren't interested. Was that a serious offer or..."

He let his question trail off, but I knew what he meant. Why didn't I want to marry Jacob? It was a question I should have asked myself more seriously the first time I turned him down instead of assuming I'd want to eventually. "It was a serious offer, but I... how much of this do you want to know?"

Charlie shrugged. "I guess as much as you want to tell me."

"Okay, so there was a guy named Jacob and we dated for a long time. He wanted to get married and I thought I wasn't ready. I thought if we were together long enough I wouldn't be able to picture my life without him. He got tired of waiting, not that I blame him, and it wasn't until after he left that I realized it wasn't time that was missing. He wasn't right for me. I don't think I really knew that until..." That was when I stopped talking. I did not say, "...until I figured out who the right guy was," because he was still technically a friend and I didn't know how he felt about our relationship anymore. Or if he was even thinking about that while grieving the loss of his grandfather. "Until much later," I said, in case Charlie was waiting for me to finish the thought. "I think it's your turn to look in the box if you're ready to move on."

He stuck his hand in the box without saying anything else. We did eventually find a match for the first blue slipper. Also a couple of noisemakers, a kitty jigsaw puzzle, a flashlight leaking battery acid and a box of purple envelopes. I did not drop the flashlight on Charlie.

When the box was empty, we stayed on the floor and talked about the rest of the weekend. Charlie was driving back to his apartment that night and then meeting family members at Andrew's house after church. They hoped to finish the packing by the end of the day. I told him I was going to have lunch with my parents as usual and then visit Riverwoods. He was surprised by that, but I thought the people there seemed so nice and that they might let me take some more pictures. We must have talked for a long time because it was late when Charlie said he should leave. I don't remember most of what we talked about, but I remember being disappointed when he left. I walked him to the door and he seemed to be carefully avoiding eye contact. I didn't know how I was supposed to signal that I wanted a goodnight kiss, but it didn't matter if he wasn't even looking for the signal.

121

Chapter 23

Mary was happy that I kept my promise to visit her again. She was sincere in her condolences, too. She took me to the dining hall where two of the same three women were having a chat. I told them how I had ordered a good camera and I needed some good subjects. They all agreed that I should come on a Bingo night. They had Bingo on Tuesdays and Thursdays. They were positive that was when I'd get the most animated shots so I agreed to come back Thursday because I didn't think I'd have my camera in time for Tuesday.

Mary took me down the hall and introduced me to a few other residents. She tried to steer me to regular Bingo players. One of them was a talk your ear off sort of person. She was very nice and I normally prefer people who let me do a lot of listening. But when I dropped in at Riverwoods, I didn't intend to spend two hours there. It was fairly late afternoon by the time I got home. I drove past Andrew's house on my way even though it wasn't on my way. Charlie's car was still parked there, next to several other cars and a big truck.

Charlie had said, "See you tomorrow," when he left my house the previous day, but we hadn't made specific plans. It felt crucial that I see him before he left town. It was the last day he planned to be at his grandfather's house. He had promised to help with my yard sale, but that was two weeks away. I was scared. It felt as though things were about to change and I didn't know if I would like the change. He seemed to have passed up a few opportunities to move our relationship out of friend territory. Had I been too subtle or was he no longer interested?

I spent a few hours trying to pretend I wasn't waiting for Charlie to call or stop by. Eventually I began to worry about missing him. I held my phone for a moment before I decided on a text message in case he was busy team-lifting a doily-covered couch. I simply said that he was welcome to stop by if he was still in town. A minute later my phone rang.

"Hi, Charlie," I said.

"Rebecca, I'm sorry it's gotten so late. It looks like we still have an hour or so of work left and we're just now trying to figure out what to do about dinner. I assume you've eaten?"

"Yeah, I did."

"I think I can eat fast and come over for just a few minutes, if that's okay with you. I have something for you."

I wasn't okay with him only staying a few minutes, but I didn't think that was what he was asking. I said, "Okay, see you soon."

He arrived at my back door with his hair matted down and his shirt sticking to his chest. There were little black flecks of something in his hair and his face was streaked with dirt and sweat. He was a fantastic sight. He immediately turned to his car, which was in my driveway with a grill sticking out of its trunk.

"I can see what you brought me," I said.

"But that's not all." Charlie motioned for me to follow.

I walked behind him and noticed what appeared to be a narrow tire track across the back of his left leg. "Did you get run over or something?"

"What?" he asked. He realized where I was looking and shook his head. "I was in the garage most of the day. Sarah found an old bike. Apparently, she hasn't ridden in a while."

I smiled at the thought of Charlie's sister chasing him on a bike. It must not have been all work down there. I asked if I could help him with the grill, but he told me to stay back so I wouldn't get my dress dirty. I had gotten in the habit of staying in my church clothes to visit at Andrew's house and I got back from Riverwoods so late anyway. I felt sort of overdressed next to Charlie.

I showed him where I planned to keep the grill. "You are going to come over here to use it, right?"

"You worried about one more thing taking up space in here?"

"No. I'm worried about you not coming over now that you don't have an excuse to be in Hartford."

Charlie let go of the grill and turned to look at me. "Do you mind being my new excuse to be in Hartford?"

I shook my head.

"Then you have nothing to worry about," he said. "Want to see what else I brought you?"

"Okay." I thought I might need to be bold and ask him how he felt about me. Saying I was an excuse to be in Hartford was a good sign. Sounding completely unconcerned about when we'd see each other again was a bad sign. He led me back to his car, warning me to keep my distance. He seemed sensitive to the fact that he needed a shower.

"It's pretty big so I don't want to get it out if you don't want it, but I found an old window air conditioner in Grandpa's garage. It still works. I thought you might want to put it in your bedroom and at least be comfortable at night."

"I think I would love that."

Charlie beamed, cute dimple perfectly visible even under a layer of dirt. "I knew you were as bothered by the heat as I was and just liked giving me a hard time."

"Maybe a little."

He took the air conditioner into the house for me and helped me set it up. Andrew had even saved the manual. As soon as the window unit was humming, Charlie said he had to go and he even started walking towards the back door.

"Wait a sec, Charlie," I said. I knew his family was waiting on his help. I didn't want him to leave though. I wanted to tell him that I loved him.

He stopped with his hand on the door. "Yeah?"

I tried to think of some excuse to keep him there while I could work up some courage. "I want to ask you two things."

"Go ahead."

"The second thing is, um, might be complicated. I don't... So the first thing is simple. Andrew had a key to my house and I guess I'll need that back now or at least should know who has it."

Charlie nodded. "Oh, okay. My mom was actually going through his keys today and said she found a few she couldn't identify. I bet one is yours. I'll make sure you get it."

"Thanks."

"What's the other thing?" he asked. He was still holding the door handle and he looked as though he couldn't get away fast enough. It wasn't the time for me to say anything significant.

"I was just thinking that the yard sale is still two weeks away and I wanted to know if there was any chance I could see you before then."

"How is that complicated?" Charlie asked. "You have to have figured out by now how much power you have over me. I will be here any time you call and ask me to come. And I'll be waiting by the phone in the meantime."

I said only, "Wow." I'm sorry that I didn't say more, but that was by far the most romantic thing anyone had ever said to me. It was so unexpected that I needed a moment to process it. Charlie didn't give me that moment.

He shook his head in frustration and mumbled, "I can't even tell if that's a good wow or a bad wow, but I need to go so we can finish and I can clean up." And then he left.

I stood there staring at the back door while I listened to his car start up and drive away. "It was a good wow," I said to myself. I was something like confused only worse because I thought I understood the situation. It was plain that Charlie was still hoping to move out of friendville and that he didn't know I had already packed his bags. I didn't think I'd been unclear. I sat next to him on the floor for hours on Saturday and never backed away. Just now he was here only a little while and I mostly talked about wanting him to come back. Maybe he thought I was a clingy friend. Or maybe he *was* ready to hear how I actually felt about him.

I stood in that same spot in my kitchen, still looking at the back door, while I considered what to do. I couldn't just blurt something out over the phone even if he did say I only had to call in order to see him. And then I knew exactly what to do. It was simple.

He didn't answer his phone. I left a message that said, "Hi, Charlie. I decided that I want to take you to dinner and that tomorrow will be soon enough. If you're interested, you should let me know what time you'll be ready after work and... um, where you live. Then I can pick you up. Bye."

I let out the breath I didn't realize I was holding as soon as I hung up. Asking someone out was a little scary even when talking to voicemail and reasonably sure the guy would say yes. I felt a bit of sympathy for anyone who had ever asked me. I also felt good about setting things right. There was nothing ambiguous about a date. Right?

I took my phone into my bedroom because it was already starting to feel cooler in there. I alternated between watching TV and watching my phone to see if Charlie was going to call me back. I gave up shortly after 11 p.m. It seemed that, unintentional or not, he was going to make me wait until morning.

I went to the kitchen to get a drink of water before I got ready for bed. Something caught my eye before I made it back to the bedroom. It was white and it was sticking through the crack just below a hinge on my front door. I pulled out an envelope with my name on it. I opened it quickly and peeked at the bottom. It was from Charlie. I folded it up before I could read anything else.

An actual pen and paper, hand-delivered letter was either really good or really bad. I wanted to savor really good while bracing myself for really bad. I couldn't do either standing barefoot in the hallway. I set the letter on my bed and brushed my teeth while I watched its reflection in the mirror. When I was ready, I climbed into bed and pulled up the sheet. I might need a thin blanket with that air conditioner. I put the letter down to get one. Back in bed I used my phone as a reading light while I held up Charlie's letter with my other hand.

> *Dear Rebecca,*
>
> *I think I owe you an apology for leaving so suddenly today. I was frustrated that we didn't have time to talk more and that I didn't know what to say. Some things are easier on paper and since you sounded sure that Grandpa's letters helped him with Rose, I figured it might be worth a try on you.*
>
> *I have to tell you that I'm struggling with what we agreed to on the 4th of July. I said I would stay only your friend unless you gave me permission for more and I have not kept up my end. I've only been pretending not to fall for you, pretending I don't fall faster every time you smile at me, pretending I don't wish every second that you felt the same. As for your part of the deal, you need to know that I'm so far gone that everything you do looks like an invitation to kiss you. I've gotten used to assuming I'm imagining things. If there's ever a time you actually want me to, you may need to be direct.*
>
> *Love,*
> *Charlie*
>
> *PS 2242 Greenlevel Rd. 6 p.m. If you show up I'm going to take that as a good sign.*

Asking Charlie's voicemail to dinner suddenly felt like a rather weak overture. I read the letter a few more times. I folded it carefully and put it on the nightstand where I'd see it if I woke up in the middle of the night. I expected to be too excited to sleep. The air conditioner provided relief from the summer heat and soothing white noise. The

126

combination contributed to the best night's sleep I'd had since moving into my house, my home.

Chapter 24

I think I ran a little faster than usual as I made my way into town Monday morning. The sun was bright and the heat felt good on my shoulders. Mabel's smile was bright, too.

"Morning, hon," she greeted me.

"Good morning to you, too."

"Charlie Tate was in here yesterday."

I nodded, wondering exactly how she was going to try to pry information from me this time.

She said, "I don't have to ask you how things are going because I asked him how he enjoyed the pizza and the boy turned about four shades of red."

"You were right that Pops does a good job," I said. I thought I'd at least pretend we were talking about pizza.

"Charlie's mama was with him," she continued. "She said he's been tight-lipped with her, too, but that she's never seen him so happy." Mabel's eyes bore into me for a moment as though she was trying to determine how I felt about Charlie being happy. When I didn't say anything, she sighed and said, "At least you won't be able to hide a ring."

I laughed. "Mabel, if Charlie gives me a ring, I promise to show it to you."

Her eyes lit up and I wished I hadn't said anything. I only meant that I wouldn't try to hide it from her and now she was probably going to tell everyone that I was hoping for a ring.

I stopped in at "Things to Do" and Jill assured me that my camera was on its way. She expected it the next afternoon, which I hoped would give me enough time to learn to use it before Thursday night Bingo.

Aiden came by to mow my lawn and he told me he had found another friend to help with the yard sale if that was okay with me. I was happy to have as many helpers as possible.

I looked up Charlie's address and found I knew exactly where it was. I had driven past that apartment complex regularly on my way to school. It was strange that he had been so close and yet I had to move to Hartford to meet him.

I was generally pretty comfortable around Charlie and I couldn't seem to remember that as I tried to find something to wear. I wanted something nicer than what I wore to sort boxes and move furniture, but not as nice as Sunday clothes. I ended up with a striped skirt and pink top. The simple choice took me forty-five minutes to make. I didn't feel any better when Charlie answered his door looking nervous, too.

"Hi," he said.

"Hi."

"Do you want to come in or should we go right away?"

"Are you hungry?" I asked.

He nodded.

"Then I guess we should go."

Charlie grabbed a set of keys from nearby and I stepped back while he came out and locked his door. He was wearing a dark green shirt that I had seen before. I loved the way it showed off his green eyes and I bet he put it on without even thinking about that. I was willing to bet he was still wearing what he wore to work.

It felt weird for me to be driving when it felt very much like a first date. The point was for the evening to feel like a date, but I thought we could skip the *first* date vibe since we already knew each other. I pulled into an Italian restaurant my parents and I liked and asked, "Is this okay?" It was the first thing either of us had said since we got in the car. I had only driven half a mile, but still.

"Yeah, I like this place."

"Have you been here much?"

"Not a lot. Usually when it's Matt's turn to pick."

I nodded because I understood. I knew that Charlie had lunch with coworkers once a week, that they took turns choosing the restaurant, and that one of them was named Matt. I knew Charlie pretty well. I knew enough about him that I should have been able to relax. We were just going to have dinner.

A server appeared to take our drink order almost as soon as we were seated in a cozy booth. When she left, I opened my menu on the table in front of me and Charlie did the same on his side. I decided what I wanted quickly and then looked up at Charlie. He was looking at me, but his eyes darted down to his menu before I could say anything.

"Charlie?"

He nodded without facing me.

"Thank you for the letter."

He brought his eyes up to mine briefly and stayed quiet. I had said the wrong thing. He told me he loved me and you don't say thank you when someone tells you he loves you. I meant to thank him for the way he said it. For once in my life I needed to make sure my feelings were not private. But then the server came back with our drinks.

"Have you decided?" she asked as she set the drinks on the table.

Charlie nodded at me. We ordered and were left alone again. I took a few slow breaths, trying to work up the nerve to say what was in my head.

"Did you see Jill this morning?" Charlie asked.

I ignored his question and kept trying to say what I needed to say, what he needed to hear.

"Rebecca? Are you okay?"

"I… I'm trying to say something and it's harder than I thought it would be."

"Oh." Charlie winced as though he was preparing for bad news. This was not going well at all. His letter was so perfect and I was ruining it.

"Charlie," I started. I figured I better start talking and then I could get it out. "I'm just sort of freaked out right now because I've been wanting to tell you something and I've never said I love you to anyone and I don't know how to do that even though I need to because I… I do."

"You do what?"

"I do… feel that way… about you."

I was staring at a shiny spot on the table while I talked, but I peeked up afterward to see if he understood. His nervous smile had been replaced by a happy one. We had a big sappy moment of looking into each other's eyes. It was a bit much for me. "I did see Jill," I said.

Charlie leaned back and let me turn down the emotional temperature. "Yeah?"

"She thinks my camera will be in tomorrow. I think I'll make muffins or something to take in when I pick it up Wednesday. I feel bad that I stopped bringing in treats when Andrew and I stopped having tea."

"I bet the guys will like that. Is her baby still in the envelope?"

"Yeah, that's a funny way to put it, but he or she is still in the envelope." Jack and Jill hadn't been able to agree on whether or not to be surprised before the ultrasound so they asked the technician to write the baby's gender on a piece of paper and seal it in an envelope. Now they were negotiating if and when they should open it.

"Do you think they're going to peek?"

"Jill says the envelope is right on the fridge where she sees it all the time. If I was her, I wouldn't have been able to hold out this long."

"Me, either," Charlie said. "You know I love surprises, but I'd be just as happy to be surprised at the ultrasound as at the birth."

As nervous as Charlie had seemed a little while ago, he sure seemed comfortable talking about a hypothetical baby. A few words from me had an amazing effect. He must not have had any idea how much I cared about him. I noticed I had calmed down as well. "I ended up staying at Riverwoods a long time yesterday," I said.

"Really? Mary talk your ear off?"

"It was mostly someone else she introduced me to. There's a lot of nice people there. They're going to let me practice with my new camera during Bingo on Thursday. Do you want to come with me?"

"Hmm... Do I want to watch you take pictures of old people playing Bingo?"

"I'll give you a hint," I said. "The answer is yes."

Charlie laughed. "Okay. Will you come get me or should I meet you there?"

"I think I better pick you up so you don't forget."

"As long as we're making fun plans... my parents want me to bring you to dinner at their house Sunday night. How do you feel about that?"

"You know what?" I said. "I have a really great idea."

"You do?" Charlie said doubtfully. He appeared to have picked up on my sarcasm.

"You know I have lunch with my parents on Sundays. Why don't you come with me in the afternoon and I'll go with you in the evening? That way we can spend almost the whole day being interrogated by our parents."

Charlie looked at me as though I had just issued some sort of dare and said, "I'm game if you are."

"All right. Why not?" It didn't really sound so bad. It mostly sounded like spending the day with Charlie. Our food arrived soon and we continued to talk while we ate. To alleviate the boredom of

131

pushing papers, some of Charlie's coworkers had begun a prank war. So far the worst that had happened to him was having all his paper clips hooked together. He was trying to stay out of it. I asked his opinion on yard sale prices. I had bought a box of little circle stickers and was trying to get everything labeled ahead of time. It was difficult to guess what someone might be willing to pay for something I didn't want for free.

I thought I'd get nervous again when we left the restaurant because of what might happen at the end of a date. We had so much fun after the initial bumps that I was more eager than anxious. When we returned to his parking lot, Charlie asked me if I wanted to come inside for a little bit. I had the guts to say exactly what I was thinking. "I think I should go home because you have to work tomorrow and I think those gray clouds are headed this way and because I just think I should." I shut off the car. "But first I'm going to get out of the car for a minute so we can say goodnight. And you should definitely come around to my side to say goodnight."

Okay, so I didn't *exactly* tell him to come over and kiss me until my toes curled. Charlie seemed to know what I meant. He walked around to where I was waiting for him with a silly grin on my face. He stopped with only a few inches between us and my grin melted in the heat that had nothing to do with the summer weather. It was a long kiss and by the end of it I wondered how I had ever thought myself capable of only tepid feelings.

Chapter 25

"B 10!" Charlie said it as loudly as he could.

Someone in the back mumbled something about not being able to hear and a woman named Edna said, "That's why there's a board you old biddy."

I heard another voice say, "She can't hear *you* either, Edna," as I took a picture of Charlie turning the drum of balls. Mary and my other new friends at Riverwoods were delighted when I brought Charlie with me. They insisted he be the guest caller for the night. They didn't even try to talk him into it, just installed him in position and explained what he had to do as though he was being given a great honor. Edna had come up and introduced herself to us as things got started. She explained that they loved having guest callers because it gave them something to complain about. A staff member was helping Charlie light up the numbers on the board and she didn't seem remotely upset to be displaced.

"Hurry up, son, some of us aren't getting any younger," a man called from the middle of the room. He was one of only two men in the room of about twenty residents. I focused my new camera on him and simply watched through the lens as I listened.

"O 71," Charlie said.

"Louder!"

"Look at the board or turn up your hearing aid," someone else said.

"Shh! I'm trying to concentrate."

Charlie called another number.

"Slow down already."

"This isn't brain surgery," said the man I was watching. "How much time do you need?"

Then I recognized Edna's voice near me. "Do you have somewhere else to be, Carl?"

Carl gave Edna something between a smirk and a sneer and I pressed the button. I looked over at Charlie as he pulled out another

133

ball. He paused for a moment and then announced the number as it appeared on the board.

"Didn't you call that already?"

"It just lit up so obviously not," someone from the crowd answered.

"How do you know it wasn't lit before?"

"My eyes still work."

Charlie called another number. It was the second game and I was amazed at his patience.

"We can't hear you, son."

"Slow down," someone else said.

"Mary, you're missing half the numbers."

"I can't help it," Mary said. "I'm too distracted."

"I know what you mean," a woman next to her agreed. "This might just be the cutest guest caller we've ever had."

The next time Charlie called a number, the woman who claimed over and over not to hear a word he said yelled, "Bingo!"

I couldn't believe he didn't look relieved. He must have hid it well. He did try to step aside before the next game and was begged to remain by all the people who had been complaining about him. He got through two more games before I finished my roll of film. I went old fashioned on the camera since I already had a digital one on my phone. I was already thinking about getting a nicer digital one as well though. We were invited to stay and play a game before we left, but we were let off the hook when we promised to come back the next week. *I* promised actually and hoped no one noticed that Charlie was intentionally quiet.

It rained while we were inside and the parking lot was steaming as we returned to it. I thought it looked like a special effect for a horror movie and I mentioned this to Charlie.

"How appropriate," he said.

"Come on, it wasn't that bad."

He stopped walking and turned to face me. His eyes were wide as though he *had* just witnessed some sort of horror and he said, "Slow down. Speed up. Slow down. We can't hear you. Slow down. Do you know how many times someone told me that the light was broken on B 6?"

I laughed. "So you're saying you're not super excited about next week?"

"Are you really coming back?"

"I said I would. And I'd like to show them the pictures I took… if they come out okay."

Charlie started walking again. "The only way I'll consider doing this again is if you call at least one game. You need to see what it's like."

"How can I take pictures from up there?"

"Just one game."

"What if instead of that I let you come over on Saturday to visit your grill?"

"That is an interesting counteroffer," he said. "I'll have to think about it."

I began fishing in my purse for my car keys. "You'll think about coming over around 4 o'clock?" I asked.

Charlie came up behind me and put his arms around my waist. I held very still while he whispered in my ear, "If you make it 3 o'clock, you'll have a deal."

Saturday he made chicken with lots of vegetables. We cut everything up into small pieces and skewered them. Then we stood by the grill together and he gave me a grilling lesson that we both knew was an excuse to hold my hand while I held the giant tongs. While we ate we prepared our strategy for spending the day with parents. Mostly this involved amusing ourselves by coming up with silly codewords. Charlie was going to say hamburger every time his mom was exaggerating a story from his past and I would say lightning bug if my dad was about to offer a lengthy speech on an economic theory. Economics had become his hobby since retiring. I did not consider that a valid hobby. Jill agreed with me and she was the expert.

Lunch with my parents was not terrible. Mom only made two comparisons to Jacob. They were both favorable, but she still deserved the look I gave her at the second one. Dad seemed to really like Charlie. They talked for quite a while about their most successful feats on a grill.

Charlie and I went to the library for a break afterwards because it was quiet and air conditioned. I checked out a few books on photography while we were there. His parents seemed so young compared to mine. They talked about the jobs from which they had not yet made plans to retire.

We drove separately since I came from Hartford and Charlie came from down the street. As we walked out to our cars together, Charlie thanked me for putting up with all the hamburgers. I laughed and told

135

him that he was the one who was exaggerating. He looked over his shoulder as we arrived at my car. I think he wanted to see if his parents were watching out the window because he said, "I don't care if they are watching," before he turned back to kiss me.

I was happy with my Bingo pictures. I put them in an album to bring with me the next Thursday. Except for one of them. It was a picture of Charlie. Though I hadn't seen it at all while we were there, the picture somehow captured the impatient glint in his eyes. It was as though I caught him in the middle of an amused sigh. I saved that picture for myself. He came with me again and tried to make the most of being pressed into service. He repeated the last number every time someone asked him to speed up. In the second game he pulled B 6 early and kept reminding them that he'd already called B 6 because he had "heard that light was out."

Charlie had at least Mary and Edna cracking up by the time he was done. When we left he asked if I now believed that he would do anything for me. I hadn't realized that had been called into question, but I told him I believed it. I also told him that I loved him. I said the actual words.

Chapter 26

It was a strange sight early on a Saturday morning. A white SUV stopped in front of my house and five teenage boys piled out of the back of it. This was my yard sale crew. I didn't recognize the woman who was driving. She waved to me as she pulled away and I waved back.

"Good morning, Ms. Hilson," Aiden said to me. I had asked him to call me Rebecca three times before I decided that must be uncomfortable for him and stopped asking. He introduced me to his friends – Ryan, Zander, Ryan and Mike. I led the guys upstairs and showed them my yard sale room.

One of the Ryans said, "Wow, that's a lot of junk." Aiden elbowed him. "I mean, stuff."

"You're right," I said. "That's why I need your help. Everything in this room, including the closet, is going to the front yard. I'll open the door at the bottom of the stairs. Just bring everything here to the yard and spread it out."

The guys all nodded at me and began grabbing their first loads. I ran ahead and propped open the side door. I had just gotten the rock wedged into the door when I heard a voice yell, "Oh, no!" This was followed by a weird clattering noise.

And then a second voice said, "Zander, you idiot!"

Several marbles arrived at the bottom of the stairs as I peeked around the corner. The guys were clustered at the top of the stairs. The one in front was holding a box sideways and several board games had spilled out and were strewn down the stairs. A few pieces of fake money were still floating to the ground.

"I'm sorry," the boy in front said. He was turning redder by the second while the rest were groaning behind him. Then I heard a knock at the front door. It was probably Charlie.

"Come in," I yelled. Then I looked up the stairs. "Okay, guys, we are off to an excellent start. If you could all help me get this back in the box, I'll sort it out while you're bringing the other things down." I

137

knelt to start picking things up from the bottom of the stairs and Charlie appeared behind me.

"I see you started without me," he said.

"They just got here."

"Yeah," said the boy I think was Mike, "it only took Zander two seconds to screw things up."

"At least it wasn't anything fragile," Aiden said.

We got all the game bits and pieces into the box and I took charge of that one. It took me a long time to find the appropriate box for each pawn, marble, chip and bit. I might have otherwise felt terrible about letting the guys do all the lifting while I supervised from the front yard though. Instead I felt terrible that Zander mumbled another apology every time he walked past me sorting the box. We (they) got everything outside by 8 a.m. Mabel told me that was the proper time to start a yard sale.

I received my first customers as the younger guys began walking towards town. They were supposed to come back at noon to help me bring in any leftovers. Charlie would stay with me the whole time. A few lamps sold early, which was good. I was most eager to unload the larger items. Jack and Jill showed up together. I thought perhaps Jill was only trying to be supportive, but she appeared genuinely interested in a few things and ended up in raptures over the old-fashioned sewing machine. She couldn't believe I was willing to part with it for so little. Charlie helped Jack get it into the back of their car.

Jill thanked us both and said, "By the way, it's a girl!"

"You peeked?"

"I finally talked her into it," Jack said proudly.

"Are you ready for a girl?"

He shook his head sadly. "I am so in over my head, but at least now we can narrow down the name choices."

"Yeah," Jill added, "we started by ruling out anything from Mother Goose. No Mary, no Betty, no Lucy..."

"And definitely no Miss Muffet." Jack kept a straight face as though Miss Muffet might have been in the running if he and Jill had less cute names.

I thanked them again for taking one of the heavier items before I helped a few other people. "Nice turnout," Mabel said as she joined a few neighbors looking over my sale.

"Yeah, thanks for helping to spread the word."

"I need a coffee table and Aiden said you had three of 'em here."

138

"Right over here." I showed her the tables. How my aunt or grandparents had managed to accumulate four coffee tables was beyond me. I was sure I could live without even one, but I was keeping the one with the marred circle anyway.

"Oh, I like this one, honey." Mabel was running her hand along the side of one of the tables. "Five bucks? If I pay you now can you put it back for me and I'll get it when I come back with the boys at noon?"

"Of course. I'll ask Charlie to put it on the porch so no one else thinks they can buy it."

"Yes, I noticed you had some good help today." Mabel looked at Charlie selling an end table to someone I didn't know and then gave me a wink before she leaned in a bit. "Listen," she said, "Dorothy James is having a competing sale down the way, but I was just there and you have way better stuff. She has almost no furniture in her sale."

I nodded, feeling a little jealous of Dorothy James. It sounded as though her leftovers would be easier to store. Mabel gushed over a few more pieces, but ended up paying me only for the coffee table. My nearest neighbor came over for a while just to chat. She ended up buying a lamp. I was very impressed with the amount of things I was giving new, better homes.

Around 11:30, I sat down on my porch steps next to Charlie. We hadn't had any customers for at least twenty minutes. Mabel told me that would happen. She said that everyone would come early even though I'd be expected to be "open" until noon.

"Guess what," I said.

Charlie lifted his eyebrows at me instead of making a guess.

"Okay, yesterday I got a call from someone at Riverwoods. Now guess."

"They fixed the light on B 6?" Charlie smirked at me.

"No, even better."

Charlie sort of half-shrugged at me. He didn't seem to want to play.

"They said that one of the residents is having a birthday party next week and that she liked my pictures so much that she wants me to come and take pictures of all her family at the party. She even offered to pay me to do it. Isn't that great?"

"That is great." He put his arm around my back and gave me a quick hug. I could tell he was genuinely happy for me, but also

139

distracted by something. I followed his gaze into my yard. There was still a lot of random stuff sitting on my lawn. Despite the good turnout and willing buyers, I had made barely enough money to cover what I was paying Aiden and his friends. Mostly I was glad that a lot of furniture had been picked up.

"I really do appreciate your help today," I said.

Charlie nodded without looking at me.

"I wish someone had taken that big chest of drawers. I know that's going to be a pain for you to bring back upstairs."

Charlie nodded again.

"I can't believe I sold all three coffee tables though."

He nodded.

"I saved that old helicopter for you to take apart later."

"Huh?" Charlie gave me a very confused look.

"I just wanted to see if you were paying attention. You seem a little, um, somewhere else."

"Oh." He drew in a long breath. "I've been thinking about Grandpa a lot."

"I know you miss him." I put my hand on his knee.

"I do, but… mostly I've been thinking about how he was a really sharp guy and sometimes he… knew things right away. I keep thinking about something he told me." Charlie reached his hand into his pocket and pulled it out as a fist. It was my turn to be confused. I thought he might be blushing a little but I wasn't sure because we had been out in the sun all morning. He focused his eyes on his hand while he kept talking. "I don't think I'm supposed to show you this first. I thought though… maybe if you knew where I was headed then you could stop me and tell me to wait if… I mean, that might be better than no… um…" Charlie glanced at me again. He was clearly nervous as he opened his hand and started fiddling with what he was holding so that I could see it. It was a ring.

"This was my grandmother's," he said. "My mom insisted that I take it when we were cleaning out Grandpa's house. I don't think she knew that I was already thinking about buying one just in case but… I guess a family one is better… I don't want to rush you, but you know the church will make us wait at least six months and I'm eager to get that started, but you probably can't even think while I'm babbling so I'll… I'll be quiet a minute to give you a chance to tell me to save it for later." Charlie stared hard at the ring he was flipping over the tip of his thumb and then off again.

140

I looked back at the chest of drawers and other items on my lawn. I didn't know what I was going to do with any of it. And there were still decisions inside my house. I had a food processor on my kitchen counter that I must have asked myself eight times if I needed or wanted. And then I looked at the profile of Charlie sitting next to me. There was no decision to wrestle with. I knew the answer to both questions without thinking. I needed him in my life and I wanted that ring on my finger. I squeezed his knee lightly and didn't say anything.

He turned to me hopefully. "I notice you're not saying anything."

I was too excited to talk so I just grinned at him.

Charlie smiled that wonderfully dimpled smile at me and said, "Okay, give me a sec." He reached into his other pocket and pulled out a piece of paper. He got down on one knee in front of me and opened the paper. He held it up in front of me to read. It said, in very nice calligraphy, "Will you marry me?"

I found enough of my voice to say, "Yes." That should not have been a surprise, but Charlie still looked relieved. He put the ring on my finger and let me keep the paper. Then he reclaimed his seat next to me and kissed me lightly. I thought I could probably handle this leaving my parents thing after all. But thinking of my parents made me realize that I needed to talk to them.

I stood up. "Wait a minute. I need to call my parents."

Charlie grabbed my hand and tried to pull me back down. "You need to call them right now?"

I pointed to the coffee table behind us. "Mabel will be back for that any minute. I can't let them find out second hand."

Charlie let go. "You're right. I better make a call, too." He pointed at the porch step. "Do you think you can meet me back here in one minute?"

I said, "I do."

~~ The End ~~

Thank you for reading *Andrew's Key*. Reviews are always appreciated.

Follow the author on Twitter @byAmandaHamm or through goodreads.com if you want to find out about future books. The next book in the *Stories From Hartford* series, *Jealousy and Yams*, is expected in April 2014.

www.ingramcontent.com/pod-product-compliance
Lightning Source LLC
Chambersburg PA
CBHW030532130626
46552CB00006B/2221